"What have you got against redheads?" Amelia asked him.

"Redheads are nothing but trouble." Braeden cocked his head at the grappling hook in her hands.

She curled her lip. "By the way, you're welcome."

"For what?"

"For saving your life."

His mouth dropped open. "You didn't…"

She pointed at the doughnut lying against the baseboard that he had been choking on minutes before.

He tightened his lips. "Thanks for saving my life, Ms. Duer."

"Don't mention it."

A bleak expression suddenly appearing in her eyes, she rubbed her temples as if she had a headache. "Dinner's at six. I'll see you then?"

"Eighteen-hundred. I'll be there."

"Don't expect haute cuisine." She cut her eyes at him, a challenge animating her face once more. "The redheaded Duers are plain and simple folks."

As she exited the cabin, he watched her disappear through the cover of trees. So that was Amelia Duer.

Tough as a sea barnacle. She'd have made a great Guardsman. He admired her strength, her ability to take care of anything life threw her way.

But who took care of her?

Lisa Carter and her family make their home in North Carolina. In addition to her Love Inspired novels, she writes romantic suspense for Abingdon Press. When she isn't writing, Lisa enjoys traveling to romantic locales, teaching writing workshops and researching her next exotic adventure. She has strong opinions on barbecue and ACC basketball. She loves to hear from readers. Connect with Lisa at lisacarterauthor.com.

Books by Lisa Carter

Love Inspired

Coast Guard Courtship

Coast Guard Courtship

Lisa Carter

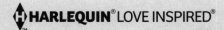

HARLEQUIN® LOVE INSPIRED®

Recycling programs
for this product may
not exist in your area.

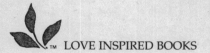

LOVE INSPIRED BOOKS

ISBN-13: 978-0-373-81833-4

Coast Guard Courtship

Copyright © 2015 by Lisa Carter

www.Harlequin.com

Printed in U.S.A.

May the God of hope fill you with all joy and peace
as you trust in him, so that you may overflow
with hope by the power of the Holy Spirit.
—*Romans* 15:13

Dedicated to the memory of Mathew Mason.
You are missed.

And to Cindy—Thanks for sharing
that Eastern Shore summer with me so long ago.

I love you.

Acknowledgments

I've taken a few liberties with the
Accomack County school calendar—
allowing Max to get out for summer early—
something for which all Accomack County
teachers can thank me for later.

Thanks to all my Onley friends who,
after all these years, still continue to welcome me
back into the peaceful harbor of
your beautiful Eastern Shore world.

Many thanks to retired United States Coast Guard
Captain Jim Umberger and Chief Petty Officer
NyxoLyno "Nick" Cangemi for answering this
civilian's seemingly endless questions about rank,
rating and protocol. You guys are the best.
Any errors are my own.

Thanks also to men and women
of the United States Coast Guard
for your dedication and sacrifice. Blessings to
you who serve on CG vessels and at CG stations.
Thank you for your service.

Miss Jean and Mr. Billy, thanks for
sharing your heart, home and family with me
again and again over these many years.
You have been a tremendous blessing in my life.

Chapter One

Bone weary after sitting up half the night with Max, Amelia closed her eyes with a sigh. The gentle blue-green waters of the tidal creek lapped against the sides of her small fishing boat. Rocked her in the soothing cradle of the waves she'd known since birth.

She savored the silence broken only by the skritching of the sand crabs on the nearby barrier island. A breeze wafted past her nose, smelling of sea salt and brine. She'd hurried this cold April morning for the chance to anchor in the crystal cove overlooking her favorite spot among the ruins of the deserted coastal village.

Amelia loved her family, her life, her home. And especially her motherless nephew, Max. But sometimes she craved the isolation of this forgotten shore. Here in the rhythm of the tide, where God most often rejuvenated her soul, she could be just Amelia.

She'd stolen this opportunity to photograph the

migratory birds in their yearly stopover on the barrier island. Images she'd transfer to her sketch pad while her charter boat clients fished during the upcoming flounder season.

Amelia had spent most of her life fishing and swimming in these waters. But Max hadn't. It'd be July before the water truly warmed. And her five-year-old nephew wasn't robust enough for even the shallow drifts of the channel.

Gripping the camera strapped about her neck, she scanned the marsh for signs of life. She peered through the cordgrass across the channel that separated the wildlife refuge from her home on the Eastern Shore of Virginia. The air hung thick with early-morning fog snaking above the dark waters of the wetlands.

Amelia's hand caught hold of the railing of the *Now I Sea* as a gust of the ever-present wind buffeted her against the side of the boat. Beyond the dunes on the other side of the island, ocean waves churned. Churned like her thoughts these days about what the doctor's report would say. About whether she and Max had another summer ahead of them to comb the beach for sea glass.

Or if time had run out.

A gaggle of birds darted upward, cawing to each other. She jerked. Her eyes swept over the rotting stumps of the island dock and the long-abandoned husks of boats moldering on the beach. She gazed across the remaining stone foundations on the sandy rise. Like the village, she'd suffered so many losses.

Please, God, not Max. Whatever You want from me, I'll do. Just please don't take Max, too.

Her Wellingtons squelched on the fiberglass deck as she padded over to the controls. She gripped the helm and, turning the ignition, brought the engine to life. Above the chugging of the motor, she pointed the bow once more toward her home in Kiptohanock. To where chores awaited, where Dad needed reminding to take his medicine, where Honey needed to be straightened out about returning to college next fall. And since Amelia's fiancé, Jordan, had died, back to the bleakness of her own possibilities.

She cast one final glance over her shoulder as the barrier island receded. One fine summer day she and Max would return here. Fourth of July, maybe. They'd have a picnic. Hunt for shells. And she'd paint the landscape to her heart's content while Max ran up and down the dunes. Happy, healthy. Whole.

One fine day... God willing. She lifted her chin and headed home.

Borne aloft on the prevailing winds, seagulls whirled in graceful figure eights above the cab of his truck. Braeden Scott kneaded the wheel, glancing out the window over the railing of the bridge, where the Chesapeake Bay sparkled like glittering diamonds in the sunshine. He gazed upward at one lone bird whose shadow hovered above his windshield.

"Just so long as you don't—"

Splat.

Great. Story of his life.

"And welcome to the Eastern Shore of Virginia to you, too, my friend." He grimaced at the whitish excrement dotting his windshield.

His Ford F-250 bumped and jolted over the last hump of the Chesapeake Bay Bridge-Tunnel, which spanned the watery distance between Virginia Beach and the Delmarva peninsula composed of parts of Virginia, Maryland and Delaware. A string of islands, shoals and spits dotted the ocean side. An archipelago, he'd been told, of uninhabited isles.

At one point in a narrow stretch along Highway 13 heading north, he sighted the bay to his left and the Atlantic on his right. Leaving Northampton County and the signs for Coast Guard Station Cape Charles behind, he crossed into Accomack County. A few miles later, he veered off the main artery at Nassawadox toward Seaside Road, per Seth Duer's instructions.

Passing fields, barns and farmhouses, he crossed the small bridge at Quinby. He skirted the hamlet of Wachapreague, hugging the shoreline, and headed toward the coastal village of Kiptohanock. He'd report for duty tomorrow to the officer in charge at the small boat station.

He drove around the village square occupied by

a cupola-topped gazebo. Not much to the fishing village. A post office. A white-steepled clapboard church. Victorian homes meandered off side lanes lined with beginning-to-leaf-out trees.

So this was Kiptohanock...

Braeden steered the nose of his truck into an empty parking slot designed for vehicles towing boats. He threw open the cab door and got out. Hands on his hips, he surveyed the marina with its aging pier, the bait store, the Sandpiper Café and the boat repair shop where he'd meet Seth and get the key to his rental. Coast Guard Station Kiptohanock hunkered just across the parking lot, with rapid-response boats tied and at the ready on an adjacent dock.

Not exactly like his last digs in Station Miami. Or even Kodiak before that.

Braeden slammed the cab door shut to silence its dinging. He consoled himself with the promise that this smaller, isolated CG station was a chance to grow his leadership skills and continue the stellar trajectory his career had been on since he'd enlisted in the United States Coast Guard a dozen years ago. A matter of killing time here before rotating out to bigger assignments.

He filled his lungs with the bracing sea air. Not so bad. Not the most exciting place he'd ever quartered, but as long as he could hear the crash of the waves, he'd do fine. And there was the added bonus of finding a furnished cabin for rent by Seth Duer, who offered free docking for his boat since the station didn't offer housing for unmarried personnel.

Braeden's first love, the sea, remained the only love in his life that hadn't let him down. Give Braeden his boat, the rhythm of the sea and, as one poet had phrased it, "a star to steer by," and he was good. Better than good. Women were trouble he didn't need in his life.

Pushing off from his truck, Braeden caught sight of an older man in jeans and a plaid shirt tinkering with a boat engine in one of the garage bays of the repair shop.

Braeden strode forward, hand outstretched. "Mr. Duer?"

The man straightened. His bristly gray brows constricted before easing as recognition dawned. His thick mustache curved upward and he thrust his hand, hard with calluses, at Braeden. "You must be Braeden Scott." Seth Duer laughed, a gravelly smoker sound. "I mean Boatswain's Mate First Class Petty Officer Braeden Scott."

Braeden smiled and shrugged. "Since you're not a Coastie and I'm not in uniform, I think we can let that bit of protocol lapse." His stomach rumbled and he reddened. "Sorry. It's been a long time since breakfast."

"Thought that might be the case." Seth nudged his chin toward a white paper bag lying next to a tool case. "One of my daughters fixed you a little snack from the Sandpiper. You haven't lived till you've had the Sandpiper's long-john doughnuts."

"One of your daughters?"

Seth grimaced. "One of my many daughters."

Braeden lifted his eyebrow.

Seth clapped a hand on his shoulder. "Maybe after you get settled into the cabin, you and I can have a quick lunch at the café and you can meet my baby girl. But first…I'd like to introduce you to a few of Kiptohanock's citizens."

They ambled past the diner toward the Kiptohanock wharf, where motorboats and small fishing vessels docked alongside the pier. Weather-beaten men paused in the midst of cleaning decks or replenishing bait buckets. Conversations halted as Braeden passed. Pink-cheeked women poked their heads out of the bait shop and joined the menfolk. In a small town like this, most everyone already knew he'd come to serve as the executive petty officer to the OIC at Station Kiptohanock.

And for those who didn't know who Braeden was, Seth Duer appeared determined to rectify the oversight. His paw clamped on to Braeden's shoulder, he introduced Braeden to each of the crusty sea dogs. A gesture Braeden appreciated.

Though their services were valued, the Guardsmen oftentimes remained outsiders in these close-knit fishing communities until given the proverbial seal of approval by a prominent local. Seth had obviously taken it upon himself to do the honors.

Might come in handy and keep tempers in check, if he ever had occasion to issue citations to any of these watermen for safety violations on their vessels. Surveying the Kiptohanock citizens, Braeden was taken aback at the many variations on a theme of red hair among the men and women both, ranging from cinnamon-coated gingers and carrot tops to full-blown titians.

Shaking his hand, the women issued invitations to the potluck after church on Sunday. But as far as God and church went, Braeden refused to commit himself. Although, he thought, giving a swift glance around the Kiptohanock square, church might be all there was to do in these parts...

Braeden sighed.

One Kiptohanock matron propped her hands on her substantial hips. "Seth Duer, your other girl is going to blow a gasket when she finds out about this here Coastie."

Seth shuffled his feet.

Braeden frowned. "Sir? What's she—?"

"Women." Seth cast a furtive look out to sea. "Don't try to understand 'em, son. May I call you son?"

Braeden nodded, dazed. He cleared his throat, wondering exactly how many daughters Seth Duer possessed. Or, rather, how many possessed him?

Either way, it promised to be an interesting living arrangement for the duration.

"Don't try to understand 'em." Seth shook his

head. "All you can do is love 'em." But he slapped Braeden on the back.

Braeden winced.

Message received loud and clear. Mess with Seth Duer's daughters, mess with Seth Duer.

"Can't tell you how glad Max and I are to have another guy on the property. We've been in dire need of more testosterone there for years." Seth pulled Braeden off the pier and back toward the repair shop.

Seth fished a brass key out of the front pocket of his faded jeans. "Here, Mr. Scott."

With some trepidation, Braeden took the key from Seth's hand. "Call me Braeden, please, Mr. Duer."

Seth smiled. "There's clean linens in the cabin. Don't forget breakfast and dinner are included at the main house. And the girls would appreciate a phone call if you won't make it for dinner."

"Yessir. I'd better get unpacked and my boat docked. I'd like to check out the lay of the land, so to speak, and meet the crew at the station, too."

"Still got those directions I emailed you? Don't forget this, either." Seth handed Braeden the white paper bag. "This ought to tide you over till that lunch we talked about."

He pronounced *tide* like "toide."

The corners of Braeden's mouth lifted, liking the lilting cadence of the local speech. He opened the bag filled with fried dough rolled in cinnamon and sugar. His nose twitched appreciatively at the aroma. He licked his lips and waved the bag. "Thanks for this."

Shore assignment. Breakfast and dinner every day sounded promising. Been years since he'd profited from home-cooked meals on a regular basis.

"You're welcome, XPO Braeden Scott." Seth gave him a two-fingered salute. "But most of all, welcome to our corner of paradise."

Braeden raised his brows as he parted from Seth and strolled toward his truck.

Paradise? Kiptohanock?

The "toide" was still out on that one.

The engine purred as she headed up the tidal creek toward home. As she rounded the neck, Amelia spotted the sailboat docked in her usual slip at the pier. Easing in the *Now I Sea*, she secured the moorings and clambered out onto the weathered gray planks of the dock. She took in the sleek hull of the vessel, its immaculate paint job and deck appearance.

Expensive...

The home port painted on the bow read Miami, Florida, and the boat was christened—she blinked once to make sure she hadn't read the name wrong—*The Trouble with Redheads*.

"Humph." She tucked an errant strand of hair behind her ear.

Who in the world?

Dad would be at the shop, Honey at the diner and Max at kindergarten. Although after last night she'd assumed—incorrectly, given Max's indignant protests at six o'clock this morning—that he'd be skipping school today.

Nowadays, people didn't usually arrive by boat, but via the road. So who…?

She grabbed hold of a long grappling hook and wended her way toward the house. Passing her Jeep, she stalked the perimeter of her home. And home to seven generations of Duers, Virginia watermen one and all.

During the past century, Northern steel magnates roughed it at the Duers' fishermen's lodge while her ancestors oystered and served as hunting guides in the winter. Crabbed and ran charters in the summer. But those days, and the steamers from Wachapreague to New York City, had long ago passed.

She rounded the corner of the two-story wraparound Victorian. Shade trees studded the front yard. She followed the property line rimmed by a white wooden fence into the trees. Light spilled from the old boat shed. A squatter? Vandals? Thieves?

Amelia's lips tightened.

Her drawings were in there. The one place where nobody in her crazy family bothered her. Her refuge during the long winter months when her problems stacked as high as crab pots and the water proved too choppy to venture from shore. Her father had always encouraged her art, but seeing it made him feel bad she'd quit school to take care of Mom, then Max and now him after his heart attack last fall.

So Amelia had confined her drawing to the boat and stashed the sketches in the abandoned boat shed. She'd spent hours laboring over each angled nuance, scale and perspective of the wildlife and people that populated her Eastern Shore world. But with taking care of Max, who was always fighting colds due to his compromised immune system, and getting ready for the upcoming charter season, she'd not had the time to indulge in her art over the past month.

Amelia set her jaw.

Those drawings belonged to her. Not great art, but they were all she had left—the drawings and Max. And she'd be keelhauled before she'd allow someone to steal what little remained of her youthful hopes and dreams.

Gripping the hooked stick, she approached the cabin. Oyster shells crunching beneath her boots, she sidled to the small porch and stretched beyond the bottom step to the second tread to avoid its telltale creak. She curled her fingers around the door handle, the metal cold against her palm. Rotating the knob, she pushed it open and held her breath.

Nothing.

Poking her head inside first and observing no sign of life, she followed with the rest of her body. The sound of running water from what had once been a kitchen drew her toward the back of the three-room structure. She pressed her spine flat against the interior wall. A faucet valve squeaked, and the sound of running water ceased.

One of the ladder-back chairs scraped away from the table she'd claimed as her art bench. Paper crackled. She closed her eyes, both hands clutching the stick, and prayed for courage.

Taking a deep breath, she lunged hook first around the door frame in an ancestor-worthy yell last heard at Gettysburg.

A man—a tall, handsome man, early thirties, whose broad shoulders tapered to the waist of his Coast Guard uniform—jolted to his feet.

The chair crashed to the floor. A long john hung from his gaping mouth. His eyes, as brown as Hershey's Kisses, were the size of sand dollars.

She jabbed the hook in his direction. "Wh-who are you? What are you doing here?"

"I'm—" He choked, the doughnut lodging in his throat. His eyes bulged. He bent over the table, gasping for air. His face turned an interesting shade of puce.

Amelia dropped the stick, letting it clatter to the floor. Stepping forward, she whacked him across the massive planes of his back.

He went into an apoplexy of hacking.

Without a second's thought, she wrapped her arms around his middle, locked her hands together at his midsection. With an upthrust, she squeezed once, then again. The doughnut sailed out of his mouth and landed with a thud against the wall.

Sputtering, he collapsed against the table. Glaring, he twisted away, sidestepping her, and in one smooth motion snatched at the stick between their feet.

Her breath hitching, she realized her mistake and dived for it at the same moment his hands grasped hold. Her hand tingled from the inadvertent contact with his, but she tugged, refusing to let go. He held on, his chest heaving.

A muscle ticked in his jaw. "Let go."

She gritted her teeth. "You let go first."

"Fine." He held both hands, palm up. "I don't know what your problem is, lady, or who you think I am, but I have a rental agreement that says I have the right to be here on a month-to-month basis. And that includes breakfast and dinner." He gestured at the table.

She stared at the key on the table, a key Dad usually kept hanging on a pegboard in the mudroom of the house. Through the window, she glimpsed a black F-250. "What's going on? Who are you?"

He pointed to the name embroidered on his Coastie-blue uniform. "Scott. Braeden Scott. Seth Duer…"

She chewed at her lip. This had her sister Honey written all over it, too. What had Honey and Dad been up to while she'd been coping with Max's treatments and keeping the business afloat?

For the first time, she became aware of the pungent aroma of fresh paint. A bouquet of daffodils graced the countertop. She fought the urge to roll her eyes.

Yep, Beatrice "Honey" Duer had been here. The Eastern Shore's own Martha Stewart wannabe.

He groaned. "Don't tell me you're the other Duer sister?"

Amelia winced.

Story of her life.

Amelia smoothed her hand down the side of her faded jeans and frowned at the encrusted fish guts. "I'm Amelia." She squared her shoulders. "And yes, I am the other Duer sister."

His eyes raked over Amelia from her marsh mud-splattered boots to the top of her head. Flushing, she skimmed stray tendrils of hair from her face and tightened her ponytail.

Once, just once, she wished she could pull off pretty like Lindi, or ultrafeminine like Honey. Anything less boyish and more womanly.

All she ever managed was "good ole buddy grungy crabber." She licked her dry lips, wishing she possessed some of Honey's lip gloss. Her eyes dropped to the floor.

Great first impression, Duer. Especially with someone so…collected? Gorgeous? Masculine?

She glanced up to find the Coastie's gaze fixed on her hair.

Her heart hammered.

Chapter Two

"What's with this place?"

Braeden ran a hand through his short-cropped hair. "Should've known you'd be another redhead."

Her eyebrows curved. "What did you say?"

Braeden folded his arms across his chest.

Amelia jabbed her thumb toward the dock. "I take it that sailboat out there is yours?"

Biting the inside of his cheek, he nodded.

"And just what have you got against redheads?"

"I think my boat speaks for itself." He cocked his head at the grappling hook in her hands. "Redheads are nothing but trouble, plain and simple."

She curled her lip. "By the way, you're welcome."

"For what?"

"For saving your life."

His mouth dropped open. "You didn't…"

She pointed at the doughnut lying against the baseboard.

He tightened his lips. "Thanks for saving my life, Ms. Duer."

"Don't mention it."

She inspected him from the top of his head to his regulation black shoes. And something in her face told him she found him wanting. Heat crept up his neck.

He clenched his jaw. "Someday I'll try to return the favor."

"Don't bother. I won't be in need of your help. As you can see, I've got my own back. Me and God."

He uncrossed his arms and took a step back.

What was with the God talk around here?

Braeden's eyes traveled over Amelia Duer—her clothing, her boots, her face.

Her hair.

Not a slave to fashion, he guessed, with her ragged-at-the-knee blue jeans tucked into the navy blue Wellingtons. And that gosh-awful neon yellow slicker, which clashed with her wind-tossed strawberry blonde hair. As he'd wrestled her for the grappling hook, the scent of seawater, mud marsh and… something else…brought the Florida Keys to mind.

Tall for a woman, with an athletic build. Late twenties, maybe. A sprinkle of freckles—the bane of redheads, in his considerable and unfortunate experience—dotted the bridge of her nose. Temper and redheaded attitude—he shot another glance at the grappling hook—in abundance.

If this was God's idea of a joke, it was a bad one

from his point of view. Good thing he preferred petite, feminine women.

A phone warbled a tune about burning kisses.

Her eyes rounded, and she fished through the pockets of her rain slicker.

Blushing, she extricated her cell. But flustered, her fingers fumbled. She dropped the phone on a phrase about love that couldn't be denied. The cell skidded across the table.

"Love, huh?" He smirked and shoved the phone in her direction. "Like *Romeo and Juliet*?"

She ignored him, seizing hold of the cell. "Honey and her pranks." She stabbed the talk button as the Pointer Sisters belted, "Fire—"

"Hello? This is—" She swung away. "Is Max okay?"

Braeden frowned at the concern lacing her voice.

"I'll be right there. Thanks for calling." Pushing the off button, she headed for the door.

Braeden caught her arm. "Is everything okay? Can I help?"

Lines of weariness carved grooves around her lovely rosebud mouth. She shook her head, the red waves coming loose, falling in soft tendrils around her face. "I'll take care of it. I need to pick up Max at school. He's not feeling—" Her face constricted. "I shouldn't have let him talk me into allowing him to go to school today."

Max?

Feeling sucker punched, he removed his hand from her arm. She had a son? A husband, too?

Duh...children and husbands usually went together, Scott.

This redhead was someone else's headache.

Which didn't make him feel any better.

He snapped his fingers. "Key lime pie." She smelled like—

"Excuse me?"

He shook his head. "Nothing."

A bleak expression in her eyes, she rubbed her temples as if she had a headache. "Dinner's at six. I'll see you then?"

"Eighteen hundred. I'll be there."

"Don't expect haute cuisine." She cut her eyes at him, a challenge animating her face once more. "The redheaded Duers are plain and simple folks."

As she exited the cabin, he followed her onto the porch, watching her disappear through the cover of trees. So that was Amelia Duer. Gutsy. Tough as a sea barnacle. She'd have made a great Guardsman. He stroked his chin, admiring her strength. Able to take care of anything life threw her way.

But who took care of her?

Rounding the square, Braeden caught sight of Seth Duer standing in front of the Sandpiper. The older man stared through the plate-glass window, shielding his eyes with his hand. Glancing at his watch, Braeden figured he had enough time to find out what was up with Amelia Duer before visiting Station Kiptohanock just across the street.

Parking, Braeden exited his truck. Gravel crunched. "Mr. Duer? Sir?"

Seth Duer jerked and whipped around. "Oh." His shoulders relaxed. "Already been to the cabin and back, huh?"

Braeden pursed his lips. "Interesting little reception committee you've got there in your older daughter, Mr. Duer. You might've warned me." He narrowed his eyes. "Or at least warned her to expect me."

Seth's eyes widened. "You met 'Melia?" He rubbed his hand over his jawline stubble. "Thought she'd be on the water till lunchtime."

"What's going on here, Mr. Duer?" Braeden rocked onto his heels. "Does our rental agreement still stand or not?"

"Course it does." Seth attempted a weak laugh. "You introduced yourselves to each other, I take it, son?"

Braeden grimaced. "Oh, yeah. Name, rank and serial number, right after she threatened me with a harpoon."

Seth's Adam's apple bobbed. "Sorry about that. 'Melia is a mite protective. And feisty."

"And potentially lethal to unwelcome visitors."

Seth swung open the glass-fronted café door. "She'll come around. She always does. Just got to give that one time."

Not to mention a wide berth, Braeden resolved as he allowed Seth to usher him inside.

"Still early for lunch, but I probably owe you a cup of joe for your trouble this morning."

After almost being skewered, Braeden reckoned Seth might owe him more than that. But he paused in the doorway, inhaling the hearty smells of eggs, fried potatoes and ham. Probably the good Smithfield, Virginia, ham he'd read about as he'd ambled up I-95. The continental thing people called breakfast at the roadside motel in Virginia Beach this morning seemed like hours ago.

He and Seth shuffled past green vinyl booths packed with some of the same men and women he'd met earlier at the marina.

"And here's my baby girl." Seth gestured toward a young blonde woman whose embroidered name on the retro 1950s waitress uniform identified her as Honey.

On second thought, maybe not so retro in Kiptohanock.

A young Guardsman leaned his elbows on the counter on either side of his coffee mug, smiling in Honey's direction.

Beside Braeden, Seth Duer went rigid.

The Guardsman grinned at Honey Duer. "Always ready... That's our motto..."

Seth growled. "Ready to chase every skirt in Kiptohanock, you mean."

The Nordic-blond Coastie swung around on the stool. His eyes narrowed.

Seth hustled Braeden forward, blocking the Guardsman's view of Honey. "This is Braeden, Honey. He's already—"

The Guardsman elbowed Braeden aside. "Hey, I was here fir—"

Braeden went ramrod stiff and broadened his shoulders. "Boatswain's Mate Third Class—" he scrutinized the surname on the fellow Coastie's uniform "—Kole. Did you just shove your XPO?"

The boy's eyes widened at the stripes on Braeden's sleeve. "Br-Brae…" His voice cracked and his sunburned features turned a color akin to eggplant. "Executive Petty Officer Braeden Scott? I didn't realize—"

Kole leaped to his feet and rammed the side of his hand into his forehead. "Boatswain's Mate Third Class Petty Officer Sawyer Kole." His blue eyes pinned a spot on the far wall above Braeden's head.

Braeden acknowledged his salute with one of his own. "At ease, Kole."

Kole spread-eagled his hips, both arms grasped behind his back.

"Just finished your two days on rotation, Kole?" Braeden studied his watch. "Or just getting ready to report to your watch this time of the morning?"

Kole—in his early twenties, Braeden wagered—

swallowed. Hard. "Yes, Petty Officer Scott. On a long-john run for the OIC."

"Then I suggest you discontinue making a public nuisance of yourself and get to Station Kiptohanock ASAP." Braeden crossed his arms. "We'll continue this conversation at the station later, and perhaps—" he blew a slow breath out from between his lips "—review CG standards for fraternization and respect for the local populace."

Kole gave a short, emphatic nod.

"Was that an affirmative, Boatswain's Mate? Do you read me?"

"Yes, Petty Officer Scott. Loud and clear. Permission to be dismissed?"

"Granted."

Snatching his cap off the counter, Kole, with a sharp pivot, exited the diner with a whoosh of air and a jingle of the bell.

Braeden angled toward his new landlord. "I'm sorr—"

Honey lobbed a napkin at her father. "Did you have to embarrass Sawyer in front of his XPO, Daddy?" She picked up Kole's abandoned fork.

Braeden stepped back.

"Now, Honey." Seth threw up his hands. "After what your sisters went through, I'm not big on Coasties."

Her brown eyes darkened. "Sawyer's not like that, Daddy."

Seth folded his arms over his chest. "They're all like that, Honey." He flung Braeden an apologetic look. "Begging your pardon, Braeden. No offense intended."

"None taken, Mr. Duer."

"Please, call me Seth." Seth swiveled to his daughter. "Honey, you know how I feel about—"

Honey dabbed her large doe eyes with the edge of her pink ruffled apron. "You're trying to ruin my life, aren't you, Dad?"

Seth's eyebrows arched. "Ruin your life? Honey…"

Guffaws bellowed from the booths.

"I'd leave it go if I were you fellows." Seth heaved a sigh, not bothering to turn his head. "Or see how quick those motors of yours get fixed." Which produced further hee-haws from Seth's gray-haired peers at the corner booth.

Seth leaned over the counter. "Braeden ran into 'Melia at the cabin."

Honey sucked in a quick breath. "How'd that go?"

Braeden scowled. "About as well as you'd expect at the end of a harpoon."

Honey rolled her eyes. "I'm so sorry, Mr. Scott. I'd hoped we could ease in an introduction tonight between dinner and pie."

"Braeden," he huffed. "Since if anything happens to me, I assume you two will be the ones making my funeral arrangements."

Honey shook her head. "Don't you worry. Amelia

will come around. May take some time, but she always gets on board eventually."

Braeden sighed. "That's what your father said."

Honey grabbed a coffee mug. "I'll give her a call." She reached for a nearby coffeepot warming on a burner. "You've had an eventful morning. You need a jolt of java to tide you over."

"No, thanks." Braeden held up a hand. "I'm headed to the station. And your sister got a call from Max's school. She's headed there to pick him up."

Seth's hand clenched on the back on the chair Kole had vacated.

Honey's lower lip trembled. "Was she upset?" She fingered her apron. "Of course she was upset. I mean, was she crying upset?"

Seth frowned. "'Melia doesn't cry. Never has. Was Max okay?"

Braeden threw him a long look. "She said Max wasn't feeling well." His gaze swung to Honey. Something was going on here that he didn't understand. "And no, she wasn't crying."

Seth nodded. "She'll handle it, then. Got it under control. She's not a crier."

Honey bit her lip. "Might be better if she did." Straightening her shoulders, Honey lifted the top of a glass cake stand filled with pastries. "If you won't take some coffee, why don't you help yourself to another long john, Braeden?"

The image of strawberry blonde waves of hair flashed across Braeden's mind. The gutsy, harpoon-wielding *married* Duer sister, he reminded himself. As for doughnuts?

After the near-choking incident at the cabin… too soon.

Too soon for a lot of things.

Refusing, Braeden promised to be on time for dinner and hurried toward the station, where at this point, the sea appeared more predictable than life amid the Duer clan.

Chapter Three

At Station Kiptohanock, a female seaman apprentice vacated Dispatch and ushered him into the chief petty officer's office. Braeden saluted.

Throwing down papers, the fiftysomething Thomas rose from his chair behind the utility desk and returned Braeden's salute. "At ease, Scott."

Braeden assumed the position, legs hip-width apart, hands clasped behind his back.

"Welcome to Station Kiptohanock." Thomas offered his hand. "A day early for your watch rotation. I'm pleased to have you serving here as my executive petty officer."

Braeden shook his hand. "Just wanted to stop by and say hello. Meet the duty personnel today."

"Reviewed your record." His new chief motioned toward a file folder. "Heard more about you through the chain of command."

Braeden winced. "About Florida, Chief…"

Chief Thomas waved a hand. "Good things, XPO.

Good things. We're lucky to have you here at Small Boat Station Kiptohanock, where we're tasked with search and rescue or maritime law enforcement of the recreational boating type, mainly." He laughed. "I only hope an adrenaline junkie like yourself won't be bored out of your wits."

Braeden stiffened into attention once more. "I'm here to serve you, Chief, the Guard and the public."

Thomas eyed him. "Relax, Scott. No criticism intended. Somebody at headquarters thinks highly of your skills...and your potential for command."

Braeden scrutinized Thomas. "Permission to speak freely, Chief?"

"Granted."

"Master Chief Davis was an old friend of my father's. Both from the same Alaskan fishing village near Homer. After my father died, he's made it his business to—" Braeden licked his lips, searching for the right word "—shepherd my career."

A knock sounded.

Thomas shifted his gaze over Braeden's shoulder. "Come."

Kole poked his head around the door frame. At the sight of his future XPO, Kole's face darkened. Braeden pushed back his shoulders. Thomas's gaze darted between the two men.

"I take it you and our landlocked Oklahoma Coastie have already introduced yourselves." Thomas rounded the desk and took a single sheet of paper from Kole. He scanned the document. "No mayday?"

Kole shook his head. "Wife reported them missing when her husband's boat failed to arrive in Wilmington yesterday. She's been unable to contact them by radio for several days due to the nor'easter last week."

Braeden stepped forward. His nerve endings vibrated with the familiar rush of excitement. "Chief?"

Thomas glanced up. "A twenty-eight-foot white center-console vessel with a red stripe, the *Abracadabra* has done a vanishing act. Two men aboard sailed out of Cape May, New Jersey."

Chief Thomas angled toward Kole. "Get the boat crew to increase their patrols." He strode to a nautical map of the Eastern Shore tacked onto the office wall.

"Our range of operational territory in the Virginia Inside Passage extends from the tip of Assawoman Island south to the Great Machipongo Inlet." Thomas tapped his finger at the Atlantic Ocean and drew an imaginary line.

Kole stood at attention. "The cutter *Mako* reports they spotted no sign of the *Abracadabra* or any debris field on their way to their home port in Cape May, Chief."

Thomas tensed. "Has Sector Hampton Roads notified Air Station Elizabeth City, Boatswain's Mate?"

Kole nodded. "Affirmative, Chief."

Thomas pursed his lips. "Good. Time to call out the big guns. Dismissed, Kole."

"Yes, Chief." And Kole headed out toward the radio room.

The female Coastie watch stander—Darden, Braeden noted for future reference—returned to remind the chief of his appointment at the Kiptohanock marina for the annual blessing of the fleet.

"You should attend, Scott." Thomas dismissed Darden.

Braeden pursed his lips. "Is that an order, Chief?"

Thomas favored him with a long, slow look. "No, not an order. A recommendation to get to know the locals you'll be serving. I hear you'll be staying at the Duer place."

Braeden nodded.

"Good people. Friends of mine from church. I sent your details Seth's way when I received your orders and your request for a place to dock your boat."

"Th-thank you, sir." Braeden flicked a glance in Thomas's direction. The jury was still out in his mind on the Duers, one strawberry blonde in particular.

The OIC leaned against the corner of his desk. "Shore command isn't all bad, Scott. With only a sixteen-member crew, you'll be on the watch list, too. I usually work the seven-to-four watch. But we've all learned to do more with less."

Braeden smiled. "It's the Coastie way."

He'd miss, though, the swell of the sea beneath the

deck of the last cutter to which he'd been assigned. But Station Kiptohanock would be another step toward qualifying for officer candidate school.

Thomas nodded. "Something to be said for getting home to dinner with the wife and kids every night, though."

Wife? Kids? Braeden kept his opinions to himself about relational entanglements.

Thomas snorted. "Besides, I hear command's grooming you for bigger things. But there's maybe something here they want you to learn first."

"I promise I won't let you or the Guard down, Chief."

Thomas's granite face cracked into a smile. "Fishing's good here even off the station dock all year. Summers are busy. Winters slow. I expect the people who report to Station Kiptohanock to be able to handle responsibility and take care of themselves. You do that, Scott, and you and I will get along great. You copy that?"

Braeden straightened and went into a salute. "Copy that, Chief."

Leaving Nandua Elementary and Highway 13, Amelia steered the Jeep toward Kiptohanock. She wished for a do-over in meeting a particular XPO. Or better yet, to avoid him altogether.

"What's that?" Strapped in his booster seat, Max pointed toward the marina, where a group gathered on the wharf.

Sailboats, fishing vessels and catamarans bobbed in the waters off the Kiptohanock pier. Flags fluttered in the midmorning breeze. One small boat manned by Coasties harbored alongside. OIC Thomas stood near the podium, Reverend Parks at his side.

Amelia circled the town square and slowed to give Max a better look-see. "I forgot today's when the Kiptohanock Coast Guard chief blesses the fleet—" she sniffed "—such as it is, for the start of the fishing and tourist season."

Max wriggled underneath the booster's harness. "I wanna see."

She frowned at him in the rearview mirror. "Sit still, Max. You need to go home and rest. Anybody too sick to go to school—"

"I'm not sick," he shouted. "Just tired."

She recoiled at the decibel level. "Don't yell at me, Max. I can hear you perfectly—"

"I don't need to rest." He tugged at the safety catch. "I wanna see the Coasties like my dad."

His dad… The good-for-nothing lowlife who'd deserted her sister and baby nephew.

Amelia's mouth hardened. "Stop twisting the seat belt, Max. We're going home and that's—"

Max yelled at the top of his lungs.

A sound not unlike the one she'd employed against a certain petty officer this morning. But Max's temper tantrums were a new outgrowth of the experimental treatments he'd endured over the winter.

Or, as her dad insisted, they were his attempts to test the boundaries of Amelia's parenting.

Although she supposed if she'd been subjected to as much pain as Max in his short life, she'd be mad, too.

Perhaps she already was, judging from the way she'd attacked an innocent Guardsman this morning. Sometimes she wanted to yell and scream and throw things like Max.

"When you yell like that—" she trained her eyes on the parking lot beside the diner "—I shut my ears."

He stopped, a silence so profound and sudden it was as if he'd switched off a faucet.

"We could park at the diner." She engaged the blinker, grateful for the reprieve to her nerve endings. "And watch from there."

"I didn't get to see the blessing last year, Mimi."

She squinted at him in the mirror. "No, you didn't."

"Because we were in…" He fell silent.

Putting the Jeep in Park, she swiveled to face him.

His lip trembled. "…that Hopkins hospital place."

She contemplated his impossibly blue eyes, so like her sister Lindi's.

Amelia blew out a breath. "Okay, Max. We'll—"

"Yahoo!" He fist pumped the air.

Grimacing, she suspected she'd been handled by a carrot-topped five-year-old. Slinging open her door and scrambling out, she stuck her key ring into her jeans. Amelia placed her hand on the passenger door handle as Braeden Scott reached for it, too.

"Here, let me—"

"I've got—"

Braeden retreated a pace. "Thought I'd help get you to the ceremony on time."

She crossed her arms over her ribbed gray henley shirt. "I told you I don't need your help."

A little boy pounded on the door. He smashed his face against the glass, giving his lips and eyes the appearance of a puffer fish.

She sighed. "Max…"

Braeden laughed. "And I thought I'd introduce myself to another member of the Duer clan."

"The *crazy* Duer clan."

Her lips quirked. Soft pink lips, he also noticed.

"Be my guest." She gestured. "Proceed at your own risk."

Opening the door, he leaned in and unlatched the safety harness, freeing Max from its confines. With a whoosh, Max paratrooped to the ground.

She took firm control of his shoulders. "Calm down, Max."

Her nephew squirmed, mutiny written across his face.

"This is the man I told you about, Max. He's renting the cabin from Granddad and Aunt Honey."

Braeden dropped on one knee to Max's level. His

tropical-blue trousers brushed the gravel. "Braeden Scott." He extended his hand to the boy, man to man.

Max wrapped his fingers around his hand and grinned. "I'm Max Duer."

The boy appeared small for his age. Skin and bones. Pale, with dark purple smudges etched under his eyes. Fragile...

Braeden lifted his gaze to Amelia. "Another redhead, I see." She fisted her hands on her hips and glowered at him. Braeden gave her a winsome smile. "Why, I bet you couldn't throw a rock in this place and not hit one."

"My dad was a Coastie." Max extended his index finger at Braeden's insignia with the crossed anchors. "But not a boatswain's mate like you. He was an electrician's mate."

Braeden ruffled Max's short hair. "You know a lot about the Coast Guard for someone so young. Got our hairstyle, too."

She pulled Max toward her. "It's starting to grow again after—"

"I'm going to be a Coastie one day." Max yanked free. "Like my dad."

"Not just like your dad. He—" She bit her lip and fixed her eyes on the toes of her Wellingtons.

Something was going on Braeden didn't understand. "Is your dad at sea?"

Max jutted his jaw. "He died. But I'm going to be just like him. Or maybe a rescue swimmer."

Amelia plucked at Max's arm. "Come on, Max. Aren't you in a rush to see the blessing of the fleet?" She lugged him toward the crowded dock.

Braeden fell in beside her. "At my last duty assignment, I got to drive the response boat as a coxswain." He peered out over the water, pensive. "Kind of miss the action and being a part of rescuing those in need. Now it looks as though I'll be stuck with administrative work most of the time, one of the downsides to higher rank."

Max stopped in his tracks. Amelia ran aground into him. Max's big eyes shone. "Could you teach me how to be a rescue swimmer, Mr. Scott? Mimi sometimes lets me help her drive the boat as her coxswain. But I really want to learn to dive."

She shook her head. "Max…"

"Call me Braeden, Max." He shrugged. "Aren't you too young to be thinking about that? You've got plenty of time."

Amelia flinched as if he'd struck her. Her mouth quivered. "Max doesn't even know how to swim yet." She cupped the crown of his head.

Max threw off her hand. "'Cause you won't let me learn." His eyes blazed.

"We've talked about that. You're not strong enough. Maybe next year…"

Max scowled.

She softened her tone. "Besides, the water's too cold this time of year."

"I'm not a baby," Max growled.

Braeden furrowed his brows and tried to defuse the situation. "I'm sure your mother knows—"

Max stamped his foot. "She's not my mother. My real mother's dead, too."

Hurt flickered across Amelia's features.

Max's nostrils flared. "She's my aunt Mimi and she's not the boss of me. I'm not a baby anymore."

She snatched at his sleeve as heads rotated in their direction. "We'll talk about this later at home."

Max jerked out of her grasp and huddled next to Braeden. "I want to go to the ceremony with Braeden, not you, Mimi." He didn't bother to lower his voice.

Braeden raised his brows at Amelia, seeking her direction as to his next move. She gave a tiny shake of her head. Tears welled in her eyes. "Let's not make a scene. Please, Max?"

An unfamiliar tenderness threatened to swamp Braeden's carefully constructed indifference.

Max stared Amelia down.

Her shoulders slumped. "We'd better go closer so Max can see better."

She slid Braeden an uncertain sidelong glance. "If you're sure you don't mind...or not too busy."

Braeden's pulse ratcheted a notch. "It's okay. No problem."

Amelia gazed at him with those big blue-green eyes of hers. "I'm sorry to be so much trouble on your first day."

Braeden focused for a long moment on her eyes

and processed the information he'd acquired via Max. Not his mother. Probably, therefore, judging by her lack of rings, not married.

He tamped down an irrational surge of joy.

Not that Braeden was in the market for a woman. Especially a redheaded one.

"Here, Max." Grasping him by his upper arms, Braeden heaved the little boy atop his shoulders. Max entwined his legs around Braeden's torso. "Best seat in the house, champ."

Max grinned and gave him a thumbs-up.

Chief Thomas took his place behind the podium. "Today we gather to bless these boats. We ask a blessing for those who work on them, for those who fish from these waters providing food to our country. For those who utilize these waters for recreation and pleasure."

His arm swept across the expanse toward the Coast Guard boat. "And to bless those who protect our nation and its citizens. I'm honored to be here today," Thomas intoned, "representing the United States Coast Guard." Thomas's cap visor gleamed in the sunlight. "My prayer for each of you is for fair winds..."

"And following seas," the crowd finished.

Braeden squared his shoulders.

A devout man, this OIC. Reminded Braeden of his father. And Master Chief Davis.

Braeden fidgeted. His arm brushed against

Amelia's shoulder and his heartbeat accelerated. Unsettled, he shoved his hands into his pockets.

He needed to put a cork in his unexpected attraction to the strawberry blonde. After all, he didn't do relationships. And this woman came loaded with complications.

A fortysomething man—"Reverend Parks," Amelia whispered—ambled to the podium. His voice boomed across the water.

"They're praying," Max whispered in a volume only slightly softer than a foghorn. "Everybody, bow your head."

Braeden darted his eyes at Amelia. His lips twitched. She covered her mouth with her hand before lowering her lashes.

"We pray, O Lord, for every seafarer. Grant them Your strength and protection. Keep each safe as they face the perils of the sea."

For the first time in a long while, Braeden closed his eyes in prayer.

The reverend continued, "God of unfathomable love, as boundless as the deep Your spirit hovered over at the dawn of time, hear our prayer. Protect them from the dangers of the wind and the rain. Bring each soul safely home to the true harbor of Your peace. And may the saving power of our Lord guide and protect them, for Christ's sake. Amen."

"Amen," murmured Amelia, her hands clasped.

"Amen," extolled the Kiptohanock residents.

Blond, gray, brunette—Braeden sighed—and redheads bowed in prayer together.

Safe harbor? Was there such a thing? Here in Kiptohanock?

"Amen," he whispered.

His first prayer since his father's sudden death. Braeden pondered what, exactly, God had in store for him in this tiny village on the shores of the Atlantic.

Chapter Four

The ceremony ended with the tolling of the old ship's bell mounted on the edge of the wharf. The bell rang out over the water across the assorted vessels in the harbor. One toll for each Kiptohanock waterman lost at sea.

Amelia shuddered.

Too many lost over the years. Friends of her dad's, former schoolmates. Sons, brothers, fathers, grandpas. As the sounds floated skyward beyond the white-steepled church, she positioned herself to avoid facing sweet Pauline Crockett. Amelia dug her nails into the palms of her hands, remembering their shared loss.

Braeden gave her a sharp look. "Your family makes its living from the water, too?"

"Dad taught us to respect it. To never turn our backs on it or take it for granted. He equipped us to fight for survival when pitted against it when we must. To be prepared for its changing face."

Amelia gestured toward the vessels anchored in the marina. "But every year the fleet grows smaller and the living gets harder to wrest from its depths. The crabs are overfished. The oysters infected."

She made a face. "And don't get the watermen started on the government regulations. In today's world, a true waterman must diversify. So I run the charter fishing trips since Dad got sick. He does part-time work for the boat repair shop."

Braeden quirked an eyebrow. "And Honey runs her B and B."

Her lips curled a fraction. "I suppose when you put it that way…" She patted Max's knee, perched atop Braeden's shoulders.

Broad shoulders. Able to carry heavy loads.

She shook her head at her fanciful thoughts. "Look, Max. The chief's tossing the memorial wreath into the harbor."

Max nodded. "For everybody lost at sea, like my dad."

Not like his dad. But she'd never say that to Max. Let the child keep what illusions he possessed as long as he could.

Braeden lowered Max to the ground when the ceremony concluded. The crowd dispersed. She spotted her dad shooting the breeze with his buddies, many of them serving as auxiliary volunteer support to Station Kiptohanock. Amelia tensed as the Kole boy waved to Honey from the CG boat at anchor in the harbor.

Max tugged at Braeden's hand. "Let's watch the boats go by."

Amelia caught Max's arm. "Braeden probably has things to do."

Max opened his palms. "Please, Mimi. *Please*."

Braeden adjusted his cap. "I really don't have anywhere to be until I report for watch tomorrow."

Two pairs of imploring eyes—bright blue and chocolate brown—shifted her way.

Amelia's high-minded resolve to avoid the XPO weakened. "Oh, all right. But only for a minute."

They shouldered past the clumps of chatting people milling about on the pier. Getting an earful from a come-here—anyone from elsewhere other than the Eastern Shore—her dad backpedaled as Amelia approached. She pivoted toward Honey, who ducked her head and disappeared into the café.

Cowards. She'd give them an earful and a piece of her temper for hatching this plot to rent out the cabin. They'd left her out of the loop and made her look like a fool in front of the XPO.

Amelia sighed.

Okay, she'd accomplished that feat under her own steam.

Max occupied himself by saluting as the flotilla of recreational and commercial fishing vessels chugged away toward the open water.

Braeden looped his thumbs in his duty belt. "I take it you knew nothing about the cabin rental. I'm sorry I scared you."

"I'm sorry I almost skewered you." She surveyed the sparkling water. "Money's been tight since Dad's heart attack. Honey had to drop out of college and come home. And with Max…" She cleared her throat. "They probably believed they were helping the Duer bottom line."

He leaned toward her, his gaze intent. "But this is going to add to your workload, isn't it?" His probing awareness penetrated down to the depths of her heart.

She flushed.

When he looked at her like that…

She wished she'd taken Honey's advice last week and had her hair styled. Big waste of money. For as often as not, she stuffed her hair inside a cap and let the sun and the wind have their way.

"You already run the family fishing business—"

"What's left of it these days."

"And operate a charter boat during tourist season by yourself?"

She nodded.

Braeden's cheeks lifted, turning his eyes into half-moons. "I'm impressed. You're a woman of many talents."

Max plucked at her sleeve. "It's not too cold, Mimi. Braeden and I could—"

"No, Max. It *is* too cold." She wrapped her arms around herself, wishing she'd brought a jacket. The wind off the water was cool. She should've been more vigilant.

Out of habit, she darted a glance at the horizon. Red sky this morning. "Sailor take warning. Wind's picking up."

Braeden removed his cap and plopped it on Max's head. "USCG," he read aloud. "Station Kiptohanock. Would you take care of it for me until lunch, bud?"

Max grinned. "Sure, Braeden. I'll take real good care of it." He trotted toward the end of the dock.

Braeden sniffed the air. His nose twitched, resembling a bird dog's. "Smells like chowder."

She relaxed. "The volunteer fire department's serving clam chowder and crab cakes to raise money for the Watermen Association."

"Want to get Max a bowl?" He dropped his eyes to the weathered pier and shuffled his feet. "Maybe get some for yourself, too?" The back of his neck reddened. "Save me from eating my first Shore meal alone. My treat."

A gust of wind carried his words. She imagined the gawking stares and resulting speculation around the lunch counter at the Sandpiper about the new XPO treating the old maid Duer sister to lunch.

Was this his attempt to make up for scaring the daylights out of her? She didn't usually merit attention of the male persuasion.

Probably only being nice to the kid's poor fishy aunt Mimi.

Shouting, Max made a futile grab as the wind snatched Braeden's cap off his head. The cap sailed into the air before plummeting into the choppy waters of the harbor.

Her stomach knotted. "Max, not so close to the edge."

"I'm not a baby, Mimi." He scowled as the cap drifted farther out of reach. "I promised Braeden."

His brows drawn together, Braeden took a step, hand outstretched. "It's okay, champ. No worries. I can get another—"

Dodging his hand, Max took a running leap. "It's not too cold. I'll show you."

She and Braeden realized his intent a second too late.

Fear stabbed her heart. "Max, don't."

Drawing up his knees in midair, Max landed like a cannonball in the blue-green waters. The top of his copper-colored hair disappeared beneath the waves.

She screamed. Heads jerked in her direction. Chief Thomas and the reverend came at a run.

Coughing, Max surged to the surface. His hands beat the water. His fingers strained for the cap. "Mimi!"

Sputtering on seawater, he disappeared from sight.

Without hesitation, Braeden dived into the water. With long, broad strokes, his arms ate up the distance separating him from Max. Kole tossed a life preserver off the side of the response boat.

Unable to stand by and do nothing, Amelia vaulted in to assist. As she sank, the shock of the freezing-cold water sucked the breath from her lungs. Her father cried out her name.

Oh, God, don't let my father try to save me.

In his weakened condition, they'd both drown.

Weighted by her Wellingtons, she struggled to maintain buoyancy. She reached for the life ring, but the boots acted as an anchor and pulled her downward. Fighting a riptide, she flailed at the water. The light receded, sounds muffled and the darkness deepened.

A body splashed, hurtling downward, on her left. Foaming bubbles obscured her view, but strong arms encircled her and yanked her sunward. Rotating her on her back, someone hauled her toward the pier. Treading water, her rescuer placed her hands on the rungs of the dock ladder.

"M-max…" Her teeth chattered.

"XPO's got him." In jumping off the CG patrol boat, Sawyer Kole had lost his own cap. "Can you climb the ladder?"

His ash-blond hair lay flattened and slick against his skull. "We need to get out of the way." Kole hoisted her leg into position on the rung.

Amelia swayed.

Hands reached from above. She gripped the rung above her head, gasping to regain her breath and replenish her spent store of strength. Between Kole, Thomas and her father, they managed to raise her dockside. Her knees buckled. She collapsed.

Amelia rolled onto her side. "Where's Max?"

On his knees, Seth cushioned her in his arms. "Amelia, are you all right?" His face contorted at the effort to hold his raw emotions in check.

She pushed onto her elbows as Braeden's head topped the ladder with Max clutched in a one-armed grip against his chest. Kole gathered Max as Braeden ascended the remaining rungs.

Kole deposited Max onto the warped dock boards.

Water streaming off his uniform, Braeden shouldered Kole aside to kneel beside Max. He immediately began a series of chest compressions alternating with puffs of breath.

Amelia scooted closer. Sharp splinters of wood pierced her jeans. "Max…" She stroked his lifeless cheek.

Honey rushed out of the diner. Seth hooked Honey around the waist. "Wake up, Max," Honey pleaded.

A sob caught in Amelia's throat. "Don't leave me, Max."

Please, God, no. Not him, too.

A gurgle.

Max's body spasmed. Braeden propped his head sideways as a fountain of water issued from Max's mouth.

She reached for him. "Max!"

The little boy's body convulsed as he gagged, hacking seawater.

"Mimi…" he whimpered, stretching out his hand.

Relief washed over her. *Thank You, God. Thank You.* Silent tears cascaded down her cheeks.

Amelia's arms itched to hold him closer, but unable to do more, she twined her fingers into his. Braeden elevated Max to a sitting position. Inching nearer, Max strained toward her.

"Don't cry, Mimi. Don't cry. I'm sorry. I won't ever do that again." Max cradled her face in his small, cold hands.

Amelia blanketed her arms around his shivering frame. "What would I have done if I'd lost you, Max?" she whispered into his hair.

"You won't ever get shed of me, Mimi. I promise." Max nestled into her warmth. "I'm as pesky as a sandbur and as hard to shake."

Choking on a laugh, she raised her eyes to Braeden. "God brought you here today. Thank you, Mr. Scott." Her jaw clenched. "Maybe your boat's name is right. We do seem to be causing you a lot of trouble."

An interesting look flashed across Braeden's face. "No trouble."

His eyes slid away and he dashed beads of water off his hair. He curled his fingers into a fist against his muscled thigh.

Seth extended his hand toward the dripping Sawyer Kole, still poised beside the ladder. "We owe you a debt of gratitude as well, young man."

The twentysomething Coastie contemplated Seth for a second, as if unsure of his sincerity. Blinking, he shook Seth's hand. "No problem. Always rea—" He cut his eyes over to Honey.

Amelia didn't miss the look they exchanged.

Honey's smile could've melted glacial ice caps.

And something went through Amelia. A sudden longing for something she'd not perceived lacking in her life before.

Thomas motioned toward the arriving EMTs. "We need to get him checked out at Riverside, Miss Duer."

Max's arms tightened around her. "No, Mimi," he whispered. "Not there. Not again."

She clutched Max against her chest. "I—I don't know if he…if I…" She couldn't stop her lips from trembling.

"Maybe getting the boy home would be best, Chief." Compassion melted Braeden's eyes. "I've got first-aid responder training, too. I can watch for any adverse signs, and if later we need to…"

Her heart eased. "I've had oyster stew in the Crock-Pot all morning." She gave Braeden a quick appraisal. "Are you sure, Mr. Scott?"

"It's Braeden." His eyes locked on hers. "And I'm glad to help." He extended a hand to help Amelia to her feet. "Besides, I believe a bowl of your oyster stew has my name on it."

At the cabin, Braeden peeled off his operational-duty uniform and changed into the more casual jeans he favored off duty. Opening his laptop, he shot off a quick email inquiry to Chief Thomas.

In the time it took Braeden to put on a gray USCG sweatshirt, the computer pinged with a new message from Thomas. At the chief's suggestion, Braeden put in a call to Reverend Parks, who then routed him to an auxiliary volunteer, retired to bayside Onancock. Accidentally sending his shoes skittering underneath the walnut armoire, Braeden discovered a brown portfolio case stashed in the far corner.

He positioned the case across the white chenille bedspread. Inside, he found a treasure trove of pen-and-ink sketches, a photograph clipped to the bottom left corner of each depiction. On the right corner, a signature was scrawled—"Mimi."

Grunting, he sank into the wing-back chair next to the nightstand and held each picture toward the light. Birds mostly, including the once-endangered osprey. Sea turtles. A haunting picture of an abandoned seaside village delineated in charcoal.

His breath seized at the sight of a small canvas portrait of a younger Max—he'd recognize that pug nose anywhere. Max crouched near the water's edge. The water lapped at the toes of his sneakers. His hand rested on the stern of a toy sailboat, as if in the act of launching the boat into deeper waters.

Braeden studied Amelia's carefully rendered strokes, especially the pastel of Max. Each illustration provided a tiny glimpse into her soul.

He blew out a breath. The case resting in his lap,

he gazed through the tree cover at the tiny band of water. "Definitely a woman of many talents."

Who'd probably never intended for anyone to find these sketches. Maybe why she'd so fiercely attacked her intruder this morning.

Braeden arrived at the main house with the port-folio case in hand. He let himself in through the screened porch. The aroma of simmering stew floated through the air.

"Amelia?"

He edged through the door frame. Best not to surprise that one. She might come at him this time with—

Braeden grinned.

The mind boggled at the idea of Amelia Duer with sharp kitchen weapons. He strolled into the living room and stopped in front of a photograph on the mantel over the fireplace. The stairs creaked.

"Oh, hey." Amelia descended from the second floor. "I finally persuaded Max to take a much-needed nap."

He glanced up. And his mouth went dry.

This Duer sister cleaned up well.

Her hair, still wet from the shower, flowed around her face. He admired the fit of her jeans and the glow her three-quarter-sleeved lilac blouse cast on her freshly scrubbed face.

She ought to wear lilac more often.

Braeden handed the case to her.

Amelia's face clouded. "You opened it?"

He waited for a redheaded explosion. "Sorry. I didn't mean to intrude. I was curious. I didn't realize it belonged to you. They're good." He stuffed his hands into his jeans pockets. "I mean, you're good. Are you self-taught or did you have training? Do you show at any galleries on the Shore?"

She pressed the case to her chest. "I'm not good enough for galleries."

"I think you underestimate yourself."

She shook her head. "A few art classes in high school, but I'm mostly self-taught. My mom gave me a few lessons, too, before..." Her gaze traveled to the picture on the mantel. "I'd been accepted into the Savannah School of Design—"

He whistled. "Impressive."

"But then..." She moistened her lips. "That's why it's so important Honey finish her education."

He pointed to the image of the lovely auburn-haired woman on the flat-bottomed scow the Virginia watermen favored for oystering and clamming in the shallow tidal waters. "Your mom?"

Amelia squirreled the case behind the piano. "That's us ten years ago." She ticked off the names. "Dad, Mom, Lindi—who is Max's mother and the eldest Duer sister—the pretty one."

She gestured to another sister forever captured in time, a replica of their auburn-haired mother. "Caroline—"

A college student, Braeden surmised from the Virginia Tech hoodie.

"The smart one."

He frowned at Amelia.

"You've met Honey. She was in elementary school when Mom died of ovarian cancer."

Braeden winced. A slow, painful death.

"Honey's the baby, and there's me." She veered toward the kitchen. "I'll dish out the stew."

Braeden caught hold of her wrist. "Which are you?"

She tilted her head. "I showed you. Between Caroline and Honey."

Braeden ran his thumb over her cheek.

Her blue-green eyes widened.

As deep and fathomless as the Great Machipongo Inlet.

Deep enough for a man to drown?

He lifted her chin between his thumb and forefinger. "Which are *you*? The talented one? The strong one?"

She quivered and stepped out of his reach. "Just Amelia. I'm just me."

The one who'd made a career of sacrificing everything for her family.

Something tore inside his chest. Braeden hunched his shoulders.

Amelia Duer. His exact emotional polar opposite. Since his dad's death and his fiancée's betrayal, he'd made a career out of not getting involved with anyone outside the line of duty.

Especially not with redheads like Carly.

Or Amelia Duer.

She called from the kitchen. "Coffee or sweet tea?"

"Tea, please." He followed her into the cheery yellow-and-white-tiled kitchen. "I get enough coffee when I'm on watch to float a battleship. Can I help?"

She signaled toward a drawer. "Spoons."

Amelia ladled the stew into blue crockery bowls, steam rising. "As far as the tea goes, since you hail from Alaska, I think it only fair to remind you that you're in the South." She placed the bowl on top of a yellow place mat.

"How'd you know I was born in Alaska?"

Amelia's mouth opened in an O. Closing it with a snap, she gripped the handle of a glass pitcher.

She'd taken the time—amid getting Max into bed for a nap—to look him up.

He grinned as red—a lovely color on her—crept up her neck.

She tossed her hair over her shoulder. "It's sweet."

He dragged his attention from his contemplation of her pink-tinted lips to her sea-flecked eyes. "What is?"

She shoved the pitcher into his hands. "The tea. Real sweet, if you think you can stand it."

Their fingers brushed. His heart jackhammered. She recoiled as if she'd been stung.

Braeden decided to crank up his flirting another notch. Just to see if her skin could approximate the color of her hair. For scientific purposes, of course.

He smacked his lips. "The sweeter the better."

And laughed when her color went off the charts.

Chapter Five

Rinsing the soup bowls, Amelia gazed out the kitchen window across the lawn to the water. Shorebirds wheeled over the marshy creek. The barrier island refuge shimmered like a tiny dot on the horizon.

"You've got a nice view from your cabin, too, Braeden."

He leaned against the counter. "Looks mighty good from where I'm standing."

But he wasn't looking out the window.

Her pulse palpitated like butterfly wings. Why did he keep staring at her that way? Men didn't notice her. Unless to remind her to pull her weight on the boat. Men noticed Honey.

Was he making fun of her? Setting her up to be the butt of a joke?

She edged past him to give the table a good scrub.

He pursed his lips. "Ah."

She cocked an eyebrow into a question mark.

He pointed to the soap dispenser. "Lime."

Now she was sure he mocked her. "It gets the fish smell off."

Honey smelled of flowers. She, on the other hand...

Blinking fast, she swiveled toward the table.

"Hey, I wasn't..." He cleared his throat. "I was thinking—"

"That's dangerous."

"I made a call to the Chief."

She continued scrubbing, keeping her back to him.

"To Reverend Parks, too."

She tensed.

"He recommended a fellow parishioner in Onancock who owns a heated pool."

Pivoting, she focused on him, the dishcloth hanging from her hand. "What are you talking about?"

He eyed the cloth as if it were a weapon. "Max."

She narrowed her eyes into slits. "What about Max?"

"He's surrounded by water, Amelia. It's irrespons—"

Amelia sucked in a quick breath.

Braeden held his hands, palm up. "Wrong choice of words. But you know after what happened today, he's got to get right back in the water or potentially be enslaved to a fear of it forever."

She clamped her teeth together so tightly her molars ached. "What's this got to do with you?"

"I want to teach him. On my off-watch days. Work on it this summer with him as a friend."

Summer... So far off. Maybe unreachable for Max.

Fighting the fear, Amelia seized on the next best distraction—her anger.

"Be his friend?" She snorted. "Until you're transferred to a more exciting assignment."

"Stop smothering him. It's clear he resents that." His rugged profile hardened. "Two-or three-year assignments, Amelia, and then you move on. You grew up here. You know that's the Guard way."

Amelia flung the dishcloth toward the sink. The hand-launched missile missed his head by a few inches. A few carefully calculated inches.

"What I know is after Mom died, Lindi and Caroline both went offshore. Lindi took up with this Norfolk-based Coastie who she later discovered kept a woman in every port. By the time she found out, she was pregnant with Max."

Braeden pushed the sleeves of his sweatshirt to his elbows. "Men who stray will stray whether they're military or civilian." His scowl deepened. "And as often as not, it's the home front sweetheart who Dear Johns returning sailors, soldiers and Coasties."

"That Coastie, whom Max posthumously adores, got stinking drunk one night on leave in San Diego, fell into the water and drowned his sorry self." She crossed her arms. "So Lindi came home. But two weeks shy of her due date, a drunk driver crossed the median on Highway 13 and plowed into her car."

"Amelia, I'm sorr—"

"Lindi died in my arms at Riverside Memorial after going into labor. With her last breath, she begged me to take care of Max."

"So you quit school and your dad—"

"I never made it to school. Dad went into a dark place after Mom died. And then when Lindi…"

"You stayed and took care of Max, your dad and Honey. Putting aside your own dreams."

Returning to the window, she shrugged. "That was the least of it. When Max turned three, he was diagnosed with leukemia."

For a moment, she relived that awful time.

Max shuddered with fear at the mere sight of the building where he received his chemo. She shrank inside at the memory of his pitiful cries for his Mimi not to take him into that place. How he'd begged her to go home instead.

How she'd held him down when the nurse inserted the poison into his port—

Braeden's breath hitched and Amelia realized she'd spoken out loud. To this near stranger she'd spilled the words she'd locked inside herself. Before she could react further, he strode across the room and took her into his arms.

Leaning into his firm chest, she gave in to another's comfort for once. His essence filled her senses. Tropical breezes laden with sandalwood. A delicious combination of paradise and something all Braeden Scott.

Maybe a friend?

She lacked the energy or vision to contemplate more. Hadn't she learned the hard way not to trust a Coastie—or anyone besides herself and God? Besides, men like Braeden didn't look twice at a tomboy like her.

Embarrassed, she twisted away.

Two-or three-year assignment. Here today, gone as soon as she let her guard down.

She chewed at her lower lip, smearing the pink gloss she'd borrowed from Honey's dresser.

"You're right about me smothering him. I'm just his aunt Mimi, not his mother. And *I've* become the scapegoat for his pain…" She took a ragged breath.

Braeden cradled her face in his hands. At the feel of them—strong and warm—against her skin, her heart accelerated.

She searched his features. And found honor and integrity.

"The way I see it—" his voice gentled "—Mimi is the closest thing the boy can say next to *Mama*."

Just as she had every night for the past week once they finished dinner, Amelia scudded back her chair.

"Got to check the gear for tomorrow's charter."

Braeden folded his napkin and half rose from his chair to waylay her. But too late. Amelia Duer launched from the dining room as if propelled by rocket fuel. The screen door slammed against the frame in her wake.

Honey sighed and began to clear the table.

Seth scuttled back his chair. "Care to cross wits with an old, washed-up waterman like myself, Braeden?"

Braeden reached for the now empty serving platter. "I should help Honey with the dishes."

"First off, you're not a washed-up waterman, Dad." Honey fluttered her hand. "And never you mind about the dishes, Braeden. Amelia cooked and left the kitchen pretty straight. These will go right into the dishwasher."

Max made car noises underneath the table.

Honey pulled out a chair. "Then Max and I have an appointment with the bathtub."

Max responded by using her foot as a ramp for his Matchbox car.

"What do you say?" Seth settled into a cane-bottomed chair next to a piecrust table where a game of checkers awaited.

Braeden glanced between Max and Honey.

"Go ahead," she encouraged, starting toward the kitchen. "But proceed at your own risk. This so-called washed-up waterman is actually known locally as a checkers shark."

Braeden eased into the chair opposite Seth. Zooming noises continued to emanate from the dining room.

Rubbing his hands together, Seth adjusted the pieces. "You take the red ones. I'll be black." The older man chuckled. "Best way to take the measure of a man. Squaring off in a game of skill and cunning."

Braeden raised his eyebrow a notch. "Skill and cunning?"

"Sharpens the mind, young man. Got to keep on my toes with all these females around." Seth craned his head toward the dining room. "Ain't that right, Max, my boy?"

Loud screeches were his only answer.

Three shutout games later, Braeden threw his hands up in surrender. He darted a surreptitious look at the clock on the mantel. Amelia, still a no-show. Max's bath time—amid much splashing and squawking cries for the XPO to rescue him—had come and gone.

Honey emerged, sopping wet, at the top of the stairs. She gripped pajama-clad Max's shoulder. "I've about had it up to here—" she made a swiping motion with her hand "—with Amelia punishing you and me for not telling her about—oh." Her mouth snapped shut at the sight of Braeden.

"I thought you'd abandoned ship by now." Honey tugged at Max. "Considering the unearthly howls coming from this one. He won't go to bed. Every night this week… I can't fight this or him again, Dad."

Seth gnashed his teeth. "Max…"

The boy's lower lip wobbled. "Mimi always reads me a story."

Braeden noticed the hardcover picture book tucked under Max's arm.

Honey let out a gust of air. "Mimi's not here right now, Max." She threw up her hands. "And just look at me. Just look at the mess you've made of me—not to mention the bathroom."

Braeden moved out of his chair. "I'll read Max the story. Would that be okay?" He edged toward the sofa. "Probably not be as good as Mimi, but I'll give it my best shot."

Seth shook his head. "Not your responsibility, Braeden, though I appreciate the offer."

"It's me Amelia is avoiding." Braeden shrugged. "Besides, it'll be fun hanging out with Max before he goes to bed." He cocked his head at the boy on the stairs. "You will go to bed after we read the story, won't you?"

Honey teetered on the step. He and Seth both held their breath. Max nodded. Everyone else exhaled in relief.

Seth grasped the armrests and heaved himself to his feet. "And I'm going to have a little talk with another family member of mine, one Amelia Anne Duer."

Honey paused at the landing. "She's shy around people she doesn't know, Dad. Don't be too hard on her."

Seth tucked in his shirt. "She's stubborn is what she is."

Honey sniffed. "Apples don't fall far from the tree."

Seth gave his other daughter a crooked smile. "Same could be said for you, too, baby girl."

With a cautious look, Max ventured off the stairs as Seth made for the door and his aunt sailed upstairs. Using only the tips of his fingers, Max extended the book to Braeden. And Braeden, for the first time, began to wonder what he'd gotten himself into. An only child, he'd never been good with kids.

Or maybe he'd simply never had the opportunity to learn.

"So what do we have here?" Braeden opened the storybook and smiled. "One of my favorites when I was a boy."

He was more than a little relieved to realize he knew the story. And that the boy's literary appetites didn't run to something the length of *War and Peace*. Although if he stalled long enough, perhaps Amelia would come back into the house.

Braeden patted the seat cushion beside him. "Hop on up and we'll begin."

Sticking his hand into the pocket of his pj's, Max retrieved his miniature muscle car. "Mimi makes noises when she reads."

"Noises?"

It was a story, Braeden recollected, about a plucky little sailboat exploring the deep blue sea.

Max nodded and scrambled beside Braeden. The little boy flipped past the title and copyright page. "It starts with the wind in the sails. Mimi makes wind sounds like this."

He demonstrated by sucking in his cheeks and blowing out small puffs of air. Max recited the first five lines from memory. The clean, just-bathed scent of the little boy reminded Braeden of the boy he'd once been. And of the parents who once read this same story to him.

Braeden let go of the book. "Sounds as though you don't need me to read it to you. You know it by heart."

All motion ceased. Max's eyes shot up to Braeden's. A pucker creased the ridge between his eyes. "I guess so…" His voice faded and Max looked down at the tiny car he clutched in his hand.

"But…" Braeden swallowed against the unexpected feeling. "Since it's been a long time since I read the story, maybe you and I—we—could read it together. You could coach me on the parts I've forgotten or if I don't do the sounds like Mimi."

"Really?" Max blinked at him.

"How about it?"

Max snuggled closer, and before long Braeden found himself as caught up in the story of the brave little sailboat as Max. They laughed together at the funny seagull parts. They groaned as the sailboat's timbers shivered in the midst of a typhoon and high waves.

By the time they reached the climax where the boat sighted a distant, welcoming shore, Max had curled into Braeden's lap.

"This is Mimi's favorite part." Max pointed at the page. "You'll never guess what the little boat finds."

Amelia's favorite part…

"Home." Braeden nuzzled his chin on the top of Max's now dry close-cropped curls. "The little boat finds home."

Max elbowed him in the ribs. "Oh, yeah. I forgot this was your favorite book, too."

Braeden fought a sudden sting of tears. He'd been alone so long. What was happening to him here in Kiptohanock? If Amelia Duer didn't cry, Coasties like him didn't, either. And yet…

"…and the little sailboat lived happily ever after forever and ever," Max continued without him. He underlined the last two words with a flourish. "The end."

Max smiled at him. "Happily ever after forever and ever," he repeated. "Mimi always says that's for me and for her and Granddad and Aunt Honey." He yawned. His eyes grew heavy. "And for you, Braeden, too, now that you're with us."

With *us*?

"Max, it's time to go to bed."

Braeden's heart skipped a beat at the sound of Amelia's voice.

His gaze flickered to where she stood outlined against the backdrop of the kitchen. In his musing, he hadn't heard Amelia come inside. He wondered how long she'd been listening. And watching them.

Amelia ventured farther into the living room. She held out her hand to the sleepy boy. "Time for you to dock in safe harbor for the night, too."

Closing the book, Braeden helped Max crawl down from his perch on the couch.

Amelia brushed the hair out of the boy's freckled face. She looked at Braeden across the top of Max's head.

He held the book out to Amelia. "Do you want me to carry him upstairs?"

A vein pulsed in her throat. "No. Max can make it on his own, can't you, Max?"

The small boy rubbed his cheek alongside the denim of her thigh. "Yeah. Thanks for the story, Brae—aeee." A yawn engulfed him.

Bending, Amelia hoisted Max into her arms.

He wrapped his arms around her neck. "Soon I'm going to be too heavy for you to carry, Mimi," he whispered into her hair. "I'm in kindergarten now."

Braeden's heart constricted at the look on Amelia's face. She closed her eyes and turned away.

"Wait!" Max arched toward Braeden. He shoved the muscle car at Braeden. "I've got more upstairs. But maybe tomorrow night, you and me could..." His blueberry eyes glowed with hope.

Braeden ruffled his hair. "You bet, Max. Tomorrow and the next night after that. As long as you want."

Amelia's lips tightened. "Don't make promises you can't keep, Coastie."

Braeden kept his face neutral, his voice even. "I'll think you'll find, if you're brave enough to take the chance, that I keep my promises, Amelia."

"That's the problem." Amelia readjusted her grip around her nephew. She headed for the stairs. "I'm not as brave as Max."

Chapter Six

Leaning into the pitch of the boat, Braeden gripped the cabin door frame. Coxswain-qualified Kole gunned the forty-five-foot rapid-response boat as they cleared Kiptohanock harbor. Other crewmembers readied themselves and the equipment until Kole brought them alongside the *Chimichanga*, located ten miles offshore.

The 911 distress call had originated with a local emergency dispatcher, who'd relayed the information to the watch stander on duty. The team from Station Kiptohanock had launched a few minutes later.

Chief Thomas had been generous, allowing Braeden the chance to see the crew in action. Or Thomas had sensed Braeden's internal struggle to reconcile himself to desk duty. For whatever reason, Braeden was grateful to be on the water and in action once more.

Kole maneuvered the craft through the channel,

threading the boat through the barrier islands. Braeden glanced at Kole's speed. A rugged swell sent the boat airborne for the space of a heartbeat before slamming the hull upon the face of the water.

His feet flat on the deck, Braeden flexed his knees, bracing as Kole gunned it over yet another wave. Braeden's stomach flew skyward and plummeted seconds later as the hull lurched.

Braeden fought the urge to grin at the delight etched across Sawyer Kole's craggy features. He'd yet to meet a coxswain who wasn't a speed demon. Ah, youth and its love affair with speed.

Unfortunately, youth was not a category Braeden belonged to anymore. Although early thirties hardly qualified for old man, has-been status, either. Masters of seamanship, boatswain's mates were all self-admitted adrenaline junkies. And Braeden missed taking part in every rescue call, but when the opportunity for promotion and leadership had arisen, he'd stepped up to the challenge.

Hitting the heave and roll of waves on the open ocean nearly swamped Braeden. Despite himself, he laughed. Kole threw him a cautious look.

"Maintain course." Braeden's lips quirked. "Get us there fast, but get us there alive, Boats."

A rakish grin slashed the contours of Kole's face and his shoulders relaxed a notch at the Coastie term of respect and implied affection for boatswain's mates. "You know what they used to say when I rode rodeo, Petty Officer Scott?"

Rodeo, huh? That explained a lot. Braeden prayed his sea legs kicked in soon. "No, what did they say, Boatswain's Mate Kole?"

"Go big or go home."

In the open frame of the cabin door, sea spray peppered Braeden's face. The not-like-anything-else adrenaline surged through his veins. How he loved this.

God had made Braeden Scott for this—of this one thing he'd been sure since he was no bigger than Max, on the deck of his father's Bering Sea fishing boat. Speaking of God…

With a deliberate effort, Braeden cleared his mind of everything except the mission.

"*Semper paratus*, Kole. Who knew 'always ready' first meant surviving your piloting skills?"

Kole flexed his hands around the wheel. "I'm thinking, XPO, you're loving this almost as much as me."

Braeden ran his tongue over his bottom lip. "No almost about it. What's the only thing that separates every Guardsman from a buccaneer, Kole?"

Kole cocked his head. "I don't know, Petty Officer."

Braeden snorted. "Nothing, Kole. There's a little bit of pirate in every Guardsman. Especially those with a boatswain's mate rating."

Kole and the other crewmembers chuckled. "Reckon that's about right, XPO."

Braeden peered out the window at the pewter-gray sky. With the binoculars, he scanned the horizon. Winds were strong, tide high, water choppy.

"There." He pointed starboard at the fifty-six-foot sailboat.

Kole cut back the throttle and eased as close as safety allowed. Fishing poles dangled off the sides. A woman waved her arms from the deck. Braeden turned on the bullhorn.

"This is the United States Coast Guard. We're responding to a call for assistance. We're coming aboard." Braeden followed with instructions as his crew prepared to board the vessel.

Several crewmembers hastened to throw lines and secure the response boat to the *Chimichanga*. Moments later Braeden and Seaman Apprentice Darden—trained as a first-aid responder—clambered over the side. A young woman rushed toward them.

"He's belowdecks. Collapsed. Unconscious. I can't get him to wake up. I didn't know what to do." She seized Braeden's arm and attempted to physically drag him below deck.

Braeden extricated himself from her clutches. "Ma'am…calm down. Breathe." He nudged his chin toward another team member to proceed and check it out. Darden, first-aid bag in hand, scooted past.

Reeking of alcohol, the passenger swayed.

"I know you've had a rough time. What's your name?" He captured both of her hands and urged the woman toward the captain's perch. "What's your husband's name?"

Braeden's eyes darted toward the ladder leading below, where Darden worked on the man.

"H-he's not m-my husband." The woman's teeth chattered.

Braeden spotted a windbreaker and snagged it before wrapping it around her quivering shoulders.

Darden's head, her ponytail threaded through the back band of her headgear, topped the ladder. "Just the two persons on board, Petty Officer Scott. His vitals are good. He's breathing on his own and starting to stir. No sign he injured himself when he fell."

Braeden turned toward the female passenger. "How long has he been out, ma'am?"

"I—I'm not sure." Her body trembled with delayed shock. "I wasn't feeling well. I've been seasick most of the time since we left Ocean City. He went belowdecks to get some aspirin. I heard a thump, and when he didn't reappear..." She lifted her hands.

"Does he have a medical history of seizures or heart problems we should be aware of?"

The woman shrugged. "We met last night at a dock party. He said he was on his way to Bermuda. He promised to take me as far as Hatteras."

"His name?" Braeden prompted again.

The woman's eyes widened and she clutched her abdomen.

Braeden grabbed the trash can in the corner just in time to save his shoes.

The injured man emerged five minutes later with support from Darden. Braeden helped the woman passenger transfer to the fast boat.

"We've put in a call for a sea tow of your boat into the harbor," Braeden informed the man.

The man groaned and put a hand to his head.

Darden assisted the man onto a bench in the response boat cabin. "He says he passed out from too much partying, Petty Officer Scott. Dispatch will have an ambulance waiting for us at the dock to transfer him and the lady to Riverside upon our arrival."

The female Coastie pried the woman off Braeden's arm. "She's probably suffering from dehydration, too."

Braeden left the turtle-green woman to Darden's tender ministrations. He gave the go-ahead for Kole to return to port. There'd be citations issued once they arrived. The boater had violated more than one safety protocol.

That was why alcohol and boating didn't mix. This man was lucky he'd not been stricken in the middle of nowhere. Or he'd be suffering more than a headache and a fine. Braeden wrinkled his nose. What caused a woman to go to sea with a man she hardly knew?

He patted Darden's shoulder as he passed. "Job well done."

Braeden made a point to commend each crew-member. No one appreciated what the Coast Guard did until they needed them. Last week, Air Station Elizabeth City reported that the men aboard the missing *Abracadabra* had cheered when the Jay-hawk helo came into sight. Those men had needed a miracle with their boat sinking beneath them in the cold Atlantic.

They'd gotten one, too, courtesy of the United States Coast Guard. And as for God?

Ignoring the niggling feeling that had started the day he arrived on the Eastern Shore, Braeden scanned his wristwatch. He'd go off duty once they reached the station. His stomach rumbled. He'd become spoiled since landing this assignment a few weeks ago.

Thanks to the meals courtesy of those Duer girls, he'd get soft if he wasn't careful. He licked his lips, though, remembering what Honey had hinted would be on the dinner table tonight.

He cut a look at Kole steering the boat past Par-ramore Island. No wonder the boy had fallen for the twentysomething coed. Although Braeden's personal tastes ran more to the feisty older—

Whoa. *Put the screeching brakes on that thought, Scott.* What was wrong with him?

This Coastie didn't do relationships. Been there, done that. Been burned. Only a fool opened him-self to that kind of heartbreak.

Here today, he reminded himself, gone tomorrow or at least next year, if he minded his p's and q's, toed the Coastie line and advanced out of this backwater.

And the God thing?

He glowered as the village church steeple came into view. Crewmembers leaped the remaining feet to the Kiptohanock dock to secure the lines. He and Darden helped the man and woman step onto the pier. EMTs hurried forward from the waiting ambulance.

Darden relinquished custody to the emergency medical personnel. Leaving the team to their respective responsibilities, Braeden ambled toward the station. Honey and Seth had done their best the past two Sundays to bribe him into joining them on a church pew.

So not happening.

Just as he'd make sure nothing happened between him and that spitfire Amelia for the duration of his assignment. Despite the home-cooked meals, to-die-for fishing, cozy quarters and obvious matchmaking attempts by the father and younger sister. Despite what had surged between him and Amelia in the kitchen that first day. Good thing said spitfire was immune to Coastie charms and had refused his offer to coach Max in water safety.

He raked a hand over his head, sending his cap flying off in front of his station locker. What had possessed him to get involved in the first place?

Since when did redheads possess the power to snare his heart?

Braeden spun the lock. He growled and jerked open the locker door. What was it about this place?

The metal door clattered against the wall.

What was it about these people?

He swiveled around to make sure no one had followed him into the locker room. His team would think he was crazy. He glared at the empty doorway.

Amelia Anne Duer had the potential to drive him crazy. Which settled it in Braeden's mind—no more after-dinner checkers with Seth. No more bedtime stories with Max. He'd gobble down dinner and retreat to the safety of his cabin.

These people were so...

Redheaded. Insidious. Trouble with a capital *T*.

Lucky for him, Amelia had mostly managed to avoid him thus far. Always out on a charter, checking lines, repairing nets. Returning to the house late, no matter how long he lingered. Bolting out the door this morning after no more than a cursory morning grunt.

Which was exactly what he wanted, wasn't it?

His irritation grew.

Braeden grabbed his gym bag, retrieved his cap and slammed the locker shut. He squared his shoulders and exhaled. Glad he'd gotten that straightened out.

As he exited the station, a whimper of pain drew his attention underneath the wharf.

Chapter Seven

~⌒~

Amelia inhaled a lungful of air to steady her pulse. She'd made it her business to avoid running into a certain Coastie boarder. Until this morning's awkward moment.

In spite of what she'd felt that day in the kitchen— She grimaced. *Because* of what she'd felt that day. Boatswain's Mate First Class Braeden Scott was not what she'd expected. He was so nice. So caring.

So…drop-dead gorgeous in his blue Coastie uniform.

Who pulled off drop-dead gorgeous at 6:00 a.m.? Not her, that was for sure, with her usual ratty shirt and bedraggled overalls. She wasn't girlfriend material. Never had been. And especially now, Amelia needed to remain focused.

They were so close to getting the final evaluation of Max's cancer scan after the last round of the alternative medicine. She prayed every day the report would find him in remission.

With her dad and Honey to take care of, she had no time for anything other than… What? She swallowed hard.

Amelia had no time for art. Much less time for someone so out of her reach. Her heart drummed in her chest.

She struggled to quiet her riotous yearnings for a happily-ever-after of her own. She couldn't, however, get Braeden's words out of her mind. Funny, she'd never considered Max's pet name for her the way Braeden interpreted it. She smiled at the possibility Braeden could be right.

As long as Braeden didn't touch her again, she'd be okay. Any more tenderness from him and she'd melt like those chocolate-kiss eyes of his.

She clomped across the crabgrass lawn toward the house and pummeled the screen door with her boot.

Get out of my head, Coastie.

"That you, 'Melia?"

She yanked open the door. "It's me, Dad."

The hinges squeaked and Amelia dropped onto the workbench to remove her boots. Prying them off, she padded in her stocking feet into the kitchen to find her former shipshape world in complete chaos.

Honey cooed over the most pathetic excuse for a dog Amelia had ever seen. Her dad scurried to fill one of Mom's best crockery bowls with water from the faucet. Braeden straightened from where he'd been leaning against the refrigerator.

Amelia's eyes rounded. "What in the name of Delmarva is going on here?"

Max didn't bother to look up from where he lay nose to nose beside the black Labrador on the kitchen floor.

She threw her hands in the air. "Well? Is somebody going to answer me, or what?"

The three adults suddenly found the pine floor fascinating.

"Max." She lurched toward her nephew. "Get away from that nasty, dirty dog."

The dog bared his teeth and growled.

Amelia's breath hitched.

Braeden inserted himself between her and the canine. "Now, 'Melia, before you get riled…"

Her eyes narrowed at his easy use of Dad's nickname for her. She sidestepped Braeden. The dog growled again.

She froze.

Braeden hooked one arm around her waist, and he thrust Amelia behind him. "Take it easy. Dogs don't like it when you come in as if you're ready to storm the beaches."

Seth deposited the bowl beside the dog. "Before you go blaming Braeden, it wasn't his doing. He spotted her lying underneath the wharf and stopped by the Sandpiper to inquire if anyone recognized the Lab. It was Honey and me who convinced him to bring the dog home."

Amelia peered over Braeden's muscled shoulder. "And is that Grandma Duer's county fair quilt?" She planted her hands on her hips. "Wait. Did you say *her*?"

For the first time she spied the black Lab's bulging belly. Amelia grimaced. "Don't tell me that dog's having puppies?"

Braeden dug his hands into his jeans pockets. Seth shuffled his feet. Honey pursed her lips and fiddled with her fingers.

"As if we need one more mouth to feed around here? Much less puppies? Like I need one more thing to take care—"

"Nobody asked you to take care of anything 'cept Max." Honey sniffed. "Stop being such a control freak."

Amelia whirled. "Sure, Little Miss Responsibility. Have you contacted the school registrar? Or did you miss the deadline again? Don't think I haven't heard about you chasing that good-for-nothing cowboy Coastie up and down the peninsula these past few months."

"Those gossipy old women at the Be-Lo. Got nothing better to do than rat me out." Honey leaped to her feet. "Despite what you think, you're not the boss of me or Dad. This is our house, too."

"'Cept I'll be the one cleaning up after the dog. Paying vet bills. Buying dog food." Amelia jabbed her finger in the air. "And you're correct about Max being my responsibility. You people ever think about dog germs? No way, no how that dog stays here. Much less puppies. We've come so far…"

She slumped against the corner of the table.

Braeden took hold of her elbow. She tensed.

"You're right, Amelia. I didn't think about that. We'll move the dog to my cabin. I'll take care of everything. Pay for everything. You've got enough to deal with—"

"Not a solution."

She gazed pointedly at his fingers entwined around her forearm until he removed his hand. "Max will only get attached, and then you'll leave and—"

"If you're bent on being honest here—" Honey leaned across the table "—why don't you tell Braeden the real reason you've got a problem with Coasties, Amelia?"

Amelia flinched.

Seth moved to intervene. "Don't, Honey."

Honey shook him off. "Why do you have to be this way, Amelia? It just makes everything worse."

Max squirmed upright. "Dogs know when you're being mean, Mimi." Tears tracked down his cheeks. "You never let me do anything. You never let me have anything I want. Why can't we keep this dog? I'm going to die anyway."

Amelia gasped. "No, sweetie." She shook her head. "That's not true."

Honey folded her arms across her chest and stared hard out the window. Seth massaged his hand over his chest. Amelia staggered toward Max. The dog barked.

Max flung himself at Braeden's knees. "Don't let her take my dog, Braeden. I—I need Blackie to stay. Till I'm gone..."

She stretched out her hand toward Max and let it drop to her thigh. "I won't let it be true, Max. I won't," she whispered. "Sunshine. Sea glass. Summer. Remember?"

Braeden wrapped his arms around the sobbing little boy. He raised his head and locked gazes with Amelia. The compassion in his eyes undid her. Her gaze darted between her father, Honey and Max.

Maybe they didn't need her running their lives. It wasn't as if she was doing such a great job running her own life. And what would happen once they no longer needed her? When Max no longer—

Her hand at her throat, she stumbled out the door and fled. The screen slammed into the door frame behind her.

"I'm sorry you witnessed that, son."

Braeden pulled the ladder-back chair from underneath the kitchen table. "You look like you need to sit for a spell, Seth."

Seth shook his head.

"Please. You're paler than sea foam." Braeden motioned to the chair. "Besides, I'm off duty and

I'd like to remain that way for the rest of the night, if you don't mind."

With a sigh, Seth sank into the chair. "All of us are so raw from the past two years with Max's cancer."

Braeden cocked his ear at the sounds from upstairs, where Honey attempted to get Max changed into his pajamas if he wanted to watch Blackie, the mother dog, give birth.

"All my girls responded to Marian's death in different ways."

Braeden flicked a glance into the darkened yard. Once he made sure Seth was okay, he needed to find Amelia. As far as he could tell, she worked and worried too much. Always taking care of others. And nobody seemed to be interested in taking care of Amelia.

His gut burned.

Not that she'd be open to comfort coming from a Coastie. But he had to make sure she was okay out there alone in the dark. All by herself, alone.

Braeden knew what that kind of alone felt like. He'd been a little older than Max when his mother died. And then came his dad's accident. Plus Carly's final blow a year ago.

"My eldest, Lindi, was so close to Marian. After Marian died, like the song says, Lindi went looking for love in all the wrong places." Seth slumped in the chair. "Caroline took off for college and never came home."

Seth's head bowed. "Consumed with grief, I was useless to my girls. Weak when I should've been strong. Left the raising of Honey to seventeen-year-old Amelia, my fishing buddy. My shadow. Without any sons, she did a man's job on the boat."

Except no one seemed to realize—but Braeden—that Amelia wasn't a man. He tamped down a surge of irritation.

Seth let his shoulders rise and fall. "With wide enough shoulders to take on the task of raising Max, too."

Braeden clenched his fist. *Not so wide*, he wanted to shout.

"Then Max got sick. And my heart attack. Seven rounds of chemo. If this last experimental treatment doesn't work…" The old man's lips tightened.

"'Melia's had a bad go of it." Seth hunched over the table. "She doesn't think I know about the bills. We—like most watermen—are self-insured. Thousands of dollars we owe—money well spent to save my grandson's life—but money we no longer have to repay the lien on the boat."

His eyes watered. "She doesn't think I know the boat is mortgaged to the hilt. I don't know what we'll do…" Seth scooted the chair across the hardwood floor. "And she doesn't think I know what she does when she gets a rare moment to herself."

He disappeared into the living room and reappeared with Amelia's portfolio. "She gave up so much for us. College, her dreams, love…"

Braeden's eyes shot up.

"She hides these from me so I won't feel bad. She hides her disappointments behind Max's care and mine, so she doesn't have time to feel bad for herself."

The cell in Braeden's pocket buzzed. Fishing it out, he examined the number and turned it off. Third call this week.

He could guess what Carly wanted after all this time. Thirteen months, two weeks and three days. The sales rep she dumped Braeden for had probably run out of money. She'd broken Braeden's heart, and he wasn't about to give her a second crack at it.

Braeden left Seth flipping through Amelia's drawings as he hurried into the night in search of one errant fishergirl. He found her silhouetted in the moonlight at the edge of the pier between his sailboat and the *Now I Sea*.

Amelia stiffened as the dock boards creaked. "Reckon if you're as intelligent as I take you for, you'll ditch this asylum and head for open waters."

"Stop trying to be so tough, Amelia. You sure do a lot of worrying for somebody who claims to trust God. And trying to control events and people is a job for which only God is qualified."

Amelia raised her eyebrows at him.

He laughed. "Yeah. Not the Coastie reprobate you took me for, huh? I'll have you know I occupied a certain pew every Sunday in Homer till Dad died at sea and his friend the master chief convinced me to enlist and find a new family in the Guard."

She lifted her chin. "What happened between you and God?"

He shrugged and skipped a stone across the water. "Like you, maybe too much loss too close together. Unlike you, I didn't have the support system you have in this town, your sister and father. No Max to ground me. Easier to drift and not remember what I'd lost. Rely on myself."

"So you set sail and never looked back."

He stuffed his hands in his pockets. "I reckon I did."

She sighed. "I don't think we're that different. I'm by nature a controller and worrier. Too often, I elbow God out of the equation. Fall back on relying on myself, not Him. Fear, not faith."

"But are you—" He pointed a finger at himself. "Are *we* ready to do a course correction? Raise the sail and let the wind blow us where it will?"

"I'm just so tired." She scrubbed her eyes with her fists. "I'm terrified every time Max gets a cold or a fever. Wondering if the leukemia has come back."

Braeden eased down beside her. "I know better than most that faith is way easier to talk about than to live. But trusting is less tiring than trying to control things we were never meant to."

She crossed her arms. "Exactly what are you suggesting?"

"'Melia—"

She tossed a disgruntled look at him.

He passed his hands through his hair. "Amelia, none of us know how much time we've got. Not you. Not a Coastie. Not Max."

She glared.

He held up a hand. "All I'm saying is none of us know where the next tide will take us."

"Sandbar or coral reef, most likely."

He angled toward her. "Or sunshine and sea glass. Depends on how you choose to look at it."

Amelia squinted at him. "So…what? Seize the day? Enjoy the moment?"

"Why not? None of us know what the future holds."

She kicked a crab pot with her socked foot and winced. "Nor how long a future we actually have."

"A month. Spring. A summer? Why not live it fully?"

She sighed. "You think I should let you give Max swim lessons."

"Trust, not fear, 'Melia." He rested his palm on her shoulder. "None of us are here forever. But there's no life worth living without hope, something to look forward to and live for."

She bit her lip. "This is going to involve me adopting a dog, isn't it?"

He laughed. "Or two."

"Braeden Scott, you and Max will be the death of me yet."

He stuck out his hand. "Friends?"

She ignored his outstretched hand. "You won't be here long enough to do more than cause trouble, and then you'll leave."

He jerked his thumb toward the sailboat. "You want to talk about trouble?"

She frowned. "This is one redhead who doesn't need your help."

He leaned closer until his lips could have brushed hers. An impulse getting harder to resist. "Whether you want to admit it or not, everyone needs help from time to time."

A strand of her hair lifted in the breeze off the water. "A summer of happy memories for Max?"

He fought the urge to touch her hair. "For you, too."

Something in his face must have revealed more than he meant to.

Amelia scowled. "I don't want your pity, Braeden. And I don't need you to rescue me."

Maybe she didn't need rescuing, but Braeden wondered if he did.

Chapter Eight

"You're going to have to let go of him, Amelia, if I'm going to teach him to swim."

Amelia tightened her grip around the wriggling-to-be-free kindergartner.

"Down, Mimi." Max arched his back. "I'm not a baby. Let go."

One hand on the ladder rail, one foot on the bottom step of the pool, Braeden's focus—on her—never wavered.

She shifted her flip-flops on the concrete. "Suppose the water's too cold and he gets chilled?"

"The water's perfect, Amelia. If you don't believe me, why don't you get in yourself and see."

Flushing, she set Max down and he sprinted toward the edge of the pool.

"Slow down, Max." Braeden held up his hand. "First rule, no running near the water."

Amelia dipped her big toe in the water to test it.

Braeden steered Max toward the ladder. "Both hands on the rails, bud."

"Wait."

He and Max paused, one foot on, one foot off.

"Aren't you going to put a life jacket on him? Or a flotation device?"

Braeden narrowed his eyes. "On second thought, if you're going to make a USCG-trained swimmer nervous over Max's first swim lesson, maybe you better wait outside in my truck."

"Yeah, Mimi. Leave us guys alone." Max propped his hand on his small hip and jutted it, Honey-style. "We don't need you. Braeden's got this. Go away."

She blinked. Braeden frowned. He locked eyes with Max. "Let's you and me get one thing straight, Candidate Duer. Women are to be respected, cherished and protected." Braeden threw Amelia a glance before his gaze returned to Max. "If I ever hear you disrespect your aunt Mimi or any other woman again, you can forget about swim lessons and anything else from this Coastie."

Max's eyes widened. He scowled. She held her breath, waiting for the explosion.

Braeden crossed his arms, his swimmer's shoulders bunching. "Your call, Duer."

The starch went out of her carrot-topped nephew. He drew a circle in the water with his toe. "Sorry, Mimi."

Braeden opened his arms and grabbed hold of

both side rails. "Good call, Duer. And for the record, Amelia…"

Amelia's heart skipped a beat when he said her name.

"I believe PFDs—personal flotation devices—cultivate a false sense of security. This boy lives beside the mother of all oceans. He needs to learn to respect that lady's sensibilities, too. Don't want any more Kiptohanock stunts on my watch."

His watch? Amelia's fingers played with her palm tree earring.

"I like your green swimsuit. You look like an Eastern Shore mermaid."

Her eyes darted to see if he mocked her. But his brown eyes glinted with admiration.

Flustered, she broke eye contact to tighten her ponytail. "For the record, it's teal."

A curious smile flickered across his face.

His eyes dropped to Max. "Let's get this guy comfortable with the water before we go hard-core."

Braeden eased Max into a sitting position on the step. Max shivered as the water covered his swim trunks. Clamping her hand against her thigh, Amelia bit her lip at her reflex. She wrapped her arms around herself.

"Lean against the first step, Max."

Max quivered as the water rose to chest level, but he complied.

"Good boy." Braeden patted his shoulder. "Since

you're behaving, Shore Girl, why don't you kick off those flip-flops and stay awhile, too."

Mermaid. Shore Girl.

Braeden and his funny names for her. But Amelia slipped out of her flip-flops and planted the seat of her cutoff jeans on the concrete. She dropped her legs over the side and let her feet dangle.

A hand's reach from Max, Braeden nonetheless relaxed against the tiled wall, his shoulders brushing against her bare leg.

Goose pimples—that had nothing to do with seventy-degree water—rose on her skin. She crossed her legs.

"Speaking of kicking…" With his shoulders pressed to the wall, Braeden extended his legs and demonstrated for Max.

After a few minutes of vigorous splashing from Max, Braeden smirked at her semisoaked appearance. "I think he's got the hang of it now, don't you?"

With a lazy grin, he stretched his arm out of the water and touched the tip of her nose. A single droplet trembled on his fingertip. A fleeting expression came and went across his expressive brown eyes. He took a deep breath and stopped smiling. "Amel—"

"I got water in my eyes!" Max balled his fists, digging into his eye sockets.

Amelia jumped to her feet. Braeden grabbed hold of Max's hands. "Don't rub, Max. Wipe like a windshield."

"It burns. It burns." Max bounced on the concrete step. "Mimi...help."

Amelia scurried over to the beach bag she'd left on a poolside chair. "I bought him goggles." She rummaged into the tote's cavernous depths and also withdrew Max's towel.

Braeden positioned Max in his lap and plucked the towel from Amelia. He swiped Max's eyes. "Settle down. You'll get used to it, I promise."

Amelia couldn't stop herself from pacing, but she kept her mouth shut.

Braeden sighed. "Maybe it wouldn't be a bad idea for Max to wear the goggles today. Till he gets comfortable with the water."

She dropped the goggles into his open hand and mouthed a thank-you.

Braeden adjusted the straps behind Max's head. "Better now?" He made fish-face contortions with his eyes and cheeks, flapping his hands on either side of his face like gills.

She and Max laughed. Something tightly coiled within Amelia loosened a notch.

"Looks like you, Max—" she pointed at Braeden "—the first time Braeden met you, at the blessing of the fleet, remember?"

The boy launched himself at Braeden. Braeden caught him and spun him around over the surface of the water. "Ready for the next lesson, little guy?"

Max entwined his legs around Braeden's torso and flexed his biceps. Or tried to.

Amelia stifled a grin.

"I'm going to be big and strong like you, Braeden."

Braeden held him close. "I think you can be anything you want to be, Max."

Max draped his skinny arms around Braeden's neck. "I love you, Boatswain's Mate Braeden Scott."

Amelia took a quick indrawn breath.

His brow furrowed, Braeden stared at the little boy. "I love you, too, Max Duer," he whispered.

He'd taken to lingering a spell over breakfast after Seth headed off to the boat shop and Honey took Max to school.

Leaning over the pen Seth had rigged in one corner of the small kitchen, Braeden patted Blackie, the black Lab. That had been quite a night when the puppies were born. He smiled, recalling Max's wide-eyed wonder as each of the five squirming puppies emerged. And when Braeden had assumed the role of a veterinary obstetrician, Amelia had been right there at his elbow, unable to hang back from the action.

And also despite Amelia's previously vehement declarations to the contrary, she'd been the one who'd insisted Blackie and the pups remain in the house.

"For Max's sake." And she'd given Braeden a haughty look, daring him to contradict her when he rounded his eyes at her abrupt change of plans.

At the squeak of the screen door hinges, he ambled toward the porch. Seated on a bench, Amelia placed one Wellington in the bootjack and tugged. Hearing his tread across the threshold, she lifted her head.

Tensing, he waited for her reaction to his presence on yet another morning. He didn't want to crowd her, but he couldn't seem to resist lingering over his second cup of coffee before he reported to the station each day.

She searched his face, and then her gaze dropped to his hands cradling a ceramic mug. "That cup for me?"

He leaned against the door frame. "Could be."

She shoved her other boot into the jack by way of reply. Wrenching her foot free, she found her balance before standing. "Don't you have work you need to be doing at the station?"

"Plenty of time before I'm due in." He didn't bother looking at his watch. This exchange between them had become a routine over the past week.

She held out her hand. "Cream and sugar?"

He nodded. "Cream and sugar." He handed her the cup.

She took a sip and looked at him over the rim of the mug. "You gonna get one for yourself, or am I drinking alone today?"

He relaxed. The secret fear she'd kick him out of her morning sanctuary abated a little more with each passing day. "Reckon I've got time for one more cup."

Braeden retrieved his mug. He heard the screen door swing open again and the corresponding thud when it closed. A minute later, he joined her outside on the porch steps.

Amelia inched over to give him space. She peered at his cup. "Black." She made a face.

He took a swig. "Don't need cream and sugar. I'm sweet enough."

She shook her head, but a smile teased at her lips.

Both of them were quiet with their own thoughts for a few moments. He enjoyed the companionable silence with Amelia. Not a girl who needed to chatter. He liked that about her.

She quivered beside him.

"What?"

Setting down her mug, she placed her index finger over her lips and pointed.

With a determined effort, he wrested his gaze away from her and toward the current lapping against the shoreline. His breath caught as a giant blue heron took flight over the swaying sea grass of the tidal marsh at low tide.

"Did you see?" she whispered. "Such beauty and power. *Awesome* doesn't do it justice."

His eyes riveted toward her face. "No, it doesn't."

Sensing his scrutiny, she hid her face in the mug. "Our Eastern Shore world must be pretty boring, I guess, to a globe-trotter like you."

"I kinda like knowing the names of most people in town."

Her lips twitched as a puppy yelped from inside the house. "Your fan club's calling. Thanks to Max and the puppies, I bet you know the names of everyone's dogs in Kiptohanock now, too."

"Not so boring a place." He smirked. "Not in a world populated with Max and the rest of the crazy Duer clan." He ducked his head and ran his finger around the rim of his cup. "There's a lot to be said for a place that anchors life by the moon and the tide."

He glanced up to find her eyes studying him.

She pursed her lips. "It's also a place where you can see the Milky Way and stars at night, too."

"If that's an invitation, it's definitely something I'd like to see."

Amelia flushed as red as Max's hair. "Not an invitation. Just an observation."

He frowned as she shoved off from the step and headed across the lawn toward the *Now I Sea* docked at the slip.

"Amelia," he whispered to no one but himself. "What am I going to do about you?"

Hard to court a lady with such a Coastie aversion. Had to go slow with a woman who refused to be rushed. Was he the crazy one for pursuing a strawberry blonde who'd made it clear she wanted nothing from him but friendship?

Braeden's mouth tightened. And yet sometimes when she didn't think he was paying attention, he'd catch Amelia looking at him, a tremulous expression on her face. Not unlike his own, he figured, when he had the opportunity to gaze at her. Was he fighting a losing battle?

Maybe.

Still…Braeden couldn't shake the idea of sailing with Amelia Duer one night under the stars.

Chapter Nine

Braeden made sure he maintained eye contact with Max to build the little boy's trust. After a week of swim lessons, Max was ready to put his face— minus the goggles—in the water. Bending his knees, Braeden crouched at Max's level. One hand holding the pool wall for support, Max locked gazes with Braeden and proceeded to blow water bubbles directly into Braeden's face.

The bubbles billowed up Braeden's nose.

With a grin, Braeden surged out of the water and wiped his face with his hand. "Candidate Duer," he choked. "Did you raspberry your instructor?"

Hooting, Max scrambled out of Braeden's long reach and raised himself on both arms over the concrete side. "Did you see, Mimi? I got Braeden good."

Ensconced in a lounge chair—Max wasn't the only one who'd made progress this last week— Amelia dropped the fashion magazine in her lap and applauded. "Way to go, Max. Way to take that Coastie down a peg or two and show him what a real waterman can do."

"Hey!" Braeden heaved himself onto his elbows beside Max. "I resent that remark on behalf of Coasties everywhere."

She cut her eyes at him. "You and Coasties everywhere resemble that remark."

His chest above water, Max shivered. Braeden gently squeezed his hand around the nape of Max's neck. "Great job, Candidate. If you're cold, though, maybe we should move on to the next mission."

"Wh-wh-what m-m-mission..." Max's teeth chattered.

"An underwater mission."

Max's eyes widened. And then ricocheted toward Amelia. She glanced up from the magazine and smiled.

"Mimi...?"

"Braeden's got you, Max. It's okay." She favored Braeden this time with a sweet smile.

Something warm liquefied Braeden's insides. He swallowed and choked on a lungful of pool water, sputtering. Max beat him on his back.

"Thanks, man."

Max let go of the wall and placed both hands in Braeden's.

"You won't let go?" Max flapped his feet as Braeden had taught him but didn't release Braeden's hands. "You promise if I don't like it, you'll—"

"I won't let go ever." Braeden edged them away from the security of the wall. "And the minute you want air, I'll bring you up."

Max clenched his jaw. "Okay. Let's do it."

Braeden moved an arm's length away, holding the boy afloat with his outstretched hands. Max gave him a tiny smile. The trust and love as Max's palms rested in his stole Braeden's breath, and he experienced a moment of clarity.

Kind of the way his father and mother had lived their lives in childlike trust in the safety of their Savior's hands. Anchored. And when trouble came, they weren't lost in an icy storm at sea or stolen by disease but secure in an eternal harbor. Welcomed like that plucky picture-book sailboat, home at last.

"Max—" he swallowed past the emotion clogging his throat "—you are the bravest, best boy I've ever known."

Amelia joined them at the edge of the pool.

Max kneaded Braeden's hands and threw Amelia what could only be described as a saucy look. "Well, sometimes I am. There was that puddle my puppy Ajax left when I snuck him upstairs yesterday…"

Amelia laughed. "And conveniently forgot to tell anybody about until…"

Max winked. "Until Aunt Honey stepped in it with her fancy shoes." He grinned. "You should've heard her scream."

Braeden led the boy toward deeper water, farther over Max's head. The way he felt more times than not around the boy's aunt Mimi. "Should have? I did hear her scream. All the way at the station."

Max bobbed, sucking in a huge breath. He scissored downward in a sudden move, his red head submersing. Braeden held tight to Max's fingertips. He flicked a glance at Amelia.

She shrugged. "Brave and bold. That's my Max. Nothing halfway about him." She started counting. "One, one thousand. Two, one thousand…"

Red hair floated around the orb of Max's head like crimson seaweed.

Braeden detected the tiny quiver of Max's fingers against his. He gripped the boy's hands and in a mighty heave-ho, Max surged upward. Water cascaded off his body.

Max exhaled in a gust of air. "How long, Mimi? Did you see me? How long?" He dashed water from his eyes and nose.

Amelia waggled her fingers to show him. "Five seconds, Max."

Braeden tugged him closer for a hug. "Nice going, Max."

Max's eyes shone. "Next time it'll be twenty."

Amelia rolled her eyes. "Did I mention brave, bold and insane, too?"

Braeden grinned over Max's head. "Just like a Coastie?"

Her lips quirked. "Whatever."

Over the next thirty minutes, Max progressed from twenty seconds to floating support-free.

Braeden made sure the little guy understood how to dog-paddle his way to the steps and the wall.

Braeden pushed toward the steps. "Time's up for today."

Max practiced his scissor kick. "Do we haf to go now?"

A feeling Braeden seconded. Who would have guessed a die-hard Coastie would come to consider this the highlight of his water-world week? There was a lot to be said for shore duty. Compensations, Braeden acknowledged, with a surreptitious look at the strawberry blonde on the sideline. More to life than the thrill of a drug interdiction off the Florida Keys. More than battling the freezing-cold waters of Kodiak.

Amelia lifted her shoulders and let them drop. "Your choice, Max. Thought you might want to celebrate your first underwater dive, though, with a visit to the Sugar Shack."

Max vaulted past Braeden like one of the rocket-propelled missiles from Wallops Island. "Really? Ice cream before dinner? My favorite red-white-and-blue Patriot's Dream?"

Braeden maneuvered the last step. Water streamed off his blue trunks and onto the concrete. Max huddled into the beach towel Amelia wrapped around him. "That invitation include me, Aunt Mimi? I wouldn't mind a little of that action myself."

With a smirk, Amelia handed him his own towel. "I'm not your aunt Mimi."

Braeden broadened his chest. "No, you're not."

His eyes drifted from the tendril of curls come loose from her ponytail to her sea-blue eyes. "Definitely not."

At his appraisal, a blush mounted from beneath the candy-pink blouse she wore tucked into her turned-up jeans. She fondled the pink sea-glass pendant at her throat.

Whoever said redheads shouldn't wear pink didn't know anything. Not from where he was standing.

But being Amelia, she jutted her jaw. "And as for what action you're referring to…"

He brushed the end of the towel over his face. "Why, ice cream, of course, Amelia. What did you think I meant?" Braeden crinkled his eyes at her. "Not yet an officer, but I am a gentleman."

She snorted.

He grinned. "And I'm willing to treat if you'll count me in."

Amelia folded her arms and rocked back. "I don't need your—"

He growled and slung the rolled towel around his neck. "Are we really going to rehash this again? Can't you ever take things at face value? Quit analyzing everything so deeply. Seize the day, 'Melia. Take what's being offered in the spirit of—"

"That Coastie spirit is exactly what I'm talking about." She tossed her head, setting the ponytail aquiver.

Braeden's eyes fastened onto the swaying mass

as more strands came loose to frame her face. He pondered what the sun-kissed Shore girl would look like, her tresses billowing around her tanned shoulders.

His heart racing, Braeden hung on for dear life to both ends of the towel straddling his neck. He cleared his throat and turned his attention—and thoughts—to his bare feet. "We better get a move on or Honey will have my head if we're late to supper."

At the Sugar Shack, with his ice cream cone in hand, Braeden soaked in the sun. The late-April morning chill had given way these past few days to a seasonable seventy by afternoon. Evenings after the sun dropped below the watery horizon could still be on the chilly side, but late afternoons were glorious.

His enjoyment of the peaceful simplicity of life here sort of surprised him. Made him wonder what he'd ever seen in the bright neon lights of Miami's hot spots. Made him wonder about a lot of choices he'd made.

Amelia sank down beside Braeden on the wooden picnic bench.

"Butter pecan your favorite?" Braeden ate around the rim of the cone.

She handed him a napkin. Max had found a school friend with whom to explore the adjacent playground. "I guess."

Amelia flicked a look at his melting cone. "I'd

have never taken you for a strawberry ice cream guy." She sniffed. "Knowing how you feel about people like me."

"People like you and Max and near everybody in a hundred-mile radius tend to grow on a guy."

She smiled. "Either that or we've worn you down." She smacked her lips while eating her ice cream cone. "Resistance is futile when it comes to Max."

"He's not the only one."

Braeden dabbed the napkin against Amelia's cheek.

"Oh…" She caught his hand. "Did I make a mess of myself again?"

He relinquished the napkin to her. "You may be the most put-together person I've ever met. Me, on the other hand?"

She raised her eyebrows. "Braeden Scott, boatswain's mate and coxswain, kindergarten swim instructor and dog obstetrician, doesn't do messes."

His cell vibrated on the picnic table between them. He ignored it and bit off a large hunk of ice cream. The cell bounced.

She glanced at the phone. "Aren't you going to answer that?"

He stretched out his legs and crossed his feet at the ankle. "Nope."

She edged closer when the phone buzzed again. "It could be important. Somebody from Florida. Old friend?"

"Don't have any old friends there. Not anymore. Just trouble."

Amelia cocked her head. "Ah."

He bristled. "What does *that* mean?"

She fluttered her hand. "Explains everything. Your boat. Your attitude toward redheads. Somebody with red hair like me."

"Redheaded, yeah. Like you?" He wiped his hands. "No. My former fiancée, Carly, had lots of freckles." Braeden thumbed the phone off. "A freckle for every soul she took."

Amelia rolled her eyes. She ate the last remaining bit of the waffle cone. He tossed the remainder of his cone and the napkin into a nearby trash can.

Braeden stuffed his hands into the pockets of his cargo shorts. "I came into port from patrol and found a letter. She Dear Braedened me."

Amelia touched his sleeve. "I'm sorry. She broke your heart."

"I was mad and hurt. At least at first." A line creased his brow. "I thought I was in love with her." He seized one of the stacked napkins. "Turns out that was a premature assessment from somebody with no clue what real love looked like."

He grimaced. "Carly did a number on my head. Not to mention my self-esteem. Took a sizable chunk of my ego with her, too."

Amelia bumped him with her shoulder. "Wow. I'd hate to have seen the before-Carly Coastie ego."

He laughed. "Yeah, I needed to be knocked down a peg...or two."

Amelia rounded her eyes at him. "Ya think?"

He grunted. "Probably still need taking down a few more notches..."

Amelia gave him a tiny salute. "Always ready to serve in whatever way I can, Scott."

He sprawled next to the table. "I can always count on you, Duer."

Braeden rubbed the five-o'clock stubble shadowing his jawline. "Between you and the rest of the Duer clan, not to mention a dog and her five pups, I don't think I've laughed this much or so often since..." His eyes flickered to the grass.

"Despite what you say now, I'm sorry she hurt you. You deserve better." Amelia nudged him in the ribs with her elbow. "Have I told you how grateful I am to you for helping Max learn to swim?"

Her gaze traveled to Max, fully occupied with his friend in what resembled the restaging of an epic pirate movie. She repressed a groan when Max fell on the gravel. But he jumped to his feet, his shin only skinned. He waved and resumed his mock battle.

Max, his muscles getting stronger every day and his face glowing with pink-cheeked health, had come a long way in three short weeks. So had she.

Shoulder to shoulder, Braeden jostled her back. "No worries. I'll make a Coastie out of him yet. You wait and see." His eyes danced.

"That's what I'm afraid of," she huffed.

Wait and see. Story of her life. The lab reports were due any day now. Amelia didn't know whether to feel sad or glad as the deadline loomed. Leastways, Braeden had made the weeks fly by for her and Max.

Closing her eyes, Amelia lifted her face to the sun. *Thank You, God, for this particular Coastie.*

Braeden grazed his arm against hers.

Her skin tingled, but she resisted the urge to open her eyes. She'd already spent enough time today gawking at his lean, chiseled features.

"Speaking of deserving better? No matter how often you brush off my attempts to express my admiration, Amelia, I'm in awe of how you've held your family together, taken care of Honey, your dad, the business and Max. You deserve more."

Her eyes flew open. "Don't paint me as a saint, Braeden. I've been angry, bitter, stung, enraged. You name it. I've been there." She rotated her head, trying to unkink her neck muscles. "Right now I'm stuck in the fear–slash–worry–slash–need-to-let-go-and-let-God mode."

"You've got so many people praying for you." The teasing gone from his voice, he shook his head. "Even me. Who'd have guessed that?"

If only…

What was she thinking? This acknowledged heretoday, gone-tomorrow Coastie boded no good for anyone, least of all her. After what had happened with her fiancé, Jordan Crockett, she should know better. *Did* know better than to give anyone the power to hurt her again.

"Best you know one thing up front." She pivoted to face him. "There are two kinds of people here on the Shore, Braeden."

He clamped his lips together. A muscle ticked in his cheek.

She rose. "Those who leave, like my sister Caroline. And those like me, who never will."

Chapter Ten

A week later as he braced onboard the rescue boat as it returned to harbor, Braeden scanned the Kipto-hanock waterfront for one redhead in particular, but no luck. Everyone else, though—redheaded, blond, brunette or gray—appeared to be on the scene. He gritted his teeth and lowered the binoculars.

Amelia Duer made him so mad. Made him want to…

He refused to give voice to what immediately leaped to his mind. Something that involved his lips and hers and would've earned him a grappling hook in the gut from the feisty, elusive Shore girl. Without her at the pool this week, swimming lessons hadn't been as much fun for either Max or him. Claiming a busy charter season, she'd also ducked out on early-morning coffee. He'd worn out his welcome waiting for her to return home each night.

When Kole approached the bow, with deliberate

effort Braeden forced his mind off the troublesome redhead and onto his job.

Kole squared his shoulders. "Nine thousand gallons of diesel, the captain says, but so far so good. No leakage, debris or pollution, sir."

The seventy-one-foot yacht had run aground of the breakers in the Kiptohanock channel and stuck fast. Braeden supervised the station's response team evacuation of the three-member *Nellie G* crew. With dusk imminent and an early-May thunderstorm on the horizon, a salvage ship couldn't tow the pleasure boat into harbor until morning.

Braeden monitored as his team escorted the reluctant-to-abandon-ship captain off the deck. "The pollution response trailer from Station Chincoteague will be on-site, just in case, though, right, Kole?"

"Affirmative, XPO."

"Good."

Back at the station, Braeden finished the last of the paperwork on the rescue as Kole sauntered out of the locker room. A waft of Old Spice floated past Braeden's nose. He waved a hand to clear the air. "Hot date, Kole?"

Sawyer Kole skidded to a stop. A wary look crossed his face. "Yes, Petty Officer Scott. I'm off duty now."

"Hmm."

The young boatswain's mate teetered in his cowboy boots. The upper half of his body strained with the effort not to lunge for the door. Guardsman discipline sent Kole into regulation stance, his hands behind his back.

But the cowboy Coastie's Adam's apple bobbed. "Was there something you needed, XPO?"

"I won't keep you long, I promise, Kole. But there's something I want to speak to you about. Something of a personal nature."

Kole's sun-bleached eyebrows arched. "Permission to speak freely?"

"Permission granted."

"Does this have anything to do with Honey Duer?"

"It does."

Kole flushed. "Pardon my grammar, XPO, but her and me ain't none of your business."

His chair scraping, Braeden came out from behind the desk and got inches from Kole's face. "That's where you're wrong, Kole. I've seen your record. Heard through the Coastie grapevine how you acquitted yourself at your last duty station."

Kole's eyes widened as Braeden jabbed a finger in his shirt.

"You, Kole, are under my command here, and Honey Duer, along with her entire family, is under my protection in this town."

Sawyer Kole's brow lowered into a V. "Grapevine works both ways."

Braeden gave Kole credit for guts—alongside stupidity—because Kole neither backpedaled nor apologized.

"You better think long and hard about what you plan to say next, Boatswain's Mate *Third* Class."

Kole aimed his eyes over Braeden's shoulder at the map of the Eastern Shore on the wall. "Only saying what is common knowledge among the ranks. How you exercised less-than-officer-candidate wisdom after your girl dumped you."

Braeden fumed. That wasn't exactly what had gone down the day after he received Carly's letter. But close enough.

Hurt and infuriated, he'd drowned his sorrows at a Coastie-frequented bar. Braeden had known better. He'd been raised better. But he had possessed enough sense to excuse himself from driving the boat when the distress call had come through the next morning after reporting for duty.

Braeden had known he was in no fit state, physically or emotionally, to pilot the boat and lead his crew, much less the people on board the sinking pontoon boat filled with Cuban refugees. Luckily his XPO had been there to take the wheel. Yet after heaving his guts and pride over the side of the boat, Braeden had managed to assist in the rescue effort, refusing to give in to his weakness.

And with the rest of the crew occupied in the shark-infested waters trying to save the frantic immigrants, he'd dived over the side to rescue a terrified child clinging to the body of her already drowned mother. Nightmares of the chaos that reigned that afternoon in the Keys haunted his dreams to this day. As did the cries of those none of the Guard had been able to save...

He struggled to regain his breath—and control of this junior Guardsman so very like Braeden Scott at that age.

Insubordinate. Insufferable know-it-all. Brash. Arrogant.

"The Duers are good people, Kole."

Kole's glacier-blue eyes flashed to Braeden before returning to his deadpan stare of the wall.

"Don't ruin her life, Kole. Please..."

Kole went into military stance, his heels clicking. "Could say the same thing to you. About the other one."

Braeden went rigid.

"Permission to be dismissed—" Kole's lips twisted as he threw Braeden a salute "—Chief Petty Officer *First* Class Scott?"

Braeden stared the Coastie down until Kole dropped his eyes. "I'm warning you, Kole. You hurt her, and I'll make sure you learn the real meaning of regret."

Amelia fluffed her hair. No time to dry it before the Wednesday-night church supper and prayer meeting. She'd returned the tourists on her boat to the Kiptohanock harbor and puttered home in time to scrub the fish smell off her skin and change into something more church appropriate.

Not that anyone in tiny Kiptohanock minded.

Everybody knew the score once deep-sea fishing got underway. Folks worked two or three jobs—whatever it took in the off-season—to pay the bills and make a living on the rugged coastline. And business had been brisk—a wonderful thing, praise God, considering the loan officer's last phone call—these past few weeks with flounder season kicking into high gear and charter boat cruises in high demand.

Without the financial wherewithal to hire a first mate, she was left doing all the work herself. And she'd also made it a policy to avoid Braeden over the past week. Because she liked him more than she should.

Time to shore up her emotional defenses. Because that smile of his did funny things to her heart. She was already afraid she was in way over her head.

Amelia pulled a shirt out of the closet and then discarded it in favor of another on the chance she encountered Braeden in the kitchen, where she'd left him a plate for dinner. But when Amelia headed downstairs, it was Honey who watched the driveway through the front bay window.

Pausing on the landing, Amelia crossed her arms. "Got a date, little sis?"

Honey swung around and wobbled in her black espadrilles. "What are you doing sneaking around the house?" She placed a hand over her heart and scowled. "You 'bout gave me a heart attack. I didn't hear you come home."

"Me sneaking?" Amelia frowned. "Dare I hope the reason you're skipping out on church tonight is 'cause you're meeting Debbie or Kathy or at least that nice Charlie Pruitt who's been sweet on you since high school?"

Honey tossed her hair over a bare shoulder. "Get off my case. You're not my mother."

Amelia's eyes narrowed at the halter-top blouse. Her eyes dropped to the barely there skirt. "I may not be your mother, but you're not going anywhere in that getup, miss."

Honey wrinkled her nose. "Just 'cause you live your life like a nun doesn't mean the rest of us have to."

Amelia's mouth tightened, and she moved toward her sister. "Any man that only finds you attractive in that—" she gestured "—outfit isn't worth having. You should be filling out the class registration forms if you're not going to church tonight."

Honey exploded. "Get off my case about school. Can't you get it through your stubborn head I don't want to go off-Shore? I want to stay here." She stamped her foot. "Like you."

Amelia seized hold of her sister's wrist. "Unlike me, I want you to have a future, Honey. I only want what's best—"

"You want to talk about the future, sis?" Honey wrenched free. "I've got plenty of future right here. Getting this B and B started. Classes at the community college in business and hospitality. Stuff that matters to me. Not calculus or sociology or any of the boring stuff you think is so important."

Amelia jutted her hip. "Options, Honey. What's wrong with expanding your horizons?"

"What's wrong with this horizon, Amelia?" Honey waved her hand. "Good enough for you, good enough for me. Stop trying to live out your disappointed dreams through me, through a future I don't want."

Amelia dug her fingernails into her hands to stop the angry retort that rose on her lips. Headlights swept across the driveway. Honey grabbed her purse.

But Amelia stepped between Honey and the door. "News flash—there's no Shore future to be had with a skirt-chasing Coastie."

Honey pushed past Amelia. "News flash, big sis, you threw away your chance for happiness." She flung the door wide. "I'm not throwing away mine."

Pain lanced Amelia's heart as her baby sister skipped down the wide-planked front steps and flopped into the flashy blue convertible with Sawyer Kole. White-faced with anger, Honey said something to the Guardsman. Palming the wheel, Sawyer gave Amelia a look she couldn't interpret. Hitting the accelerator, he gunned the Chevy, tires spraying gravel, toward the road where the taillights disappeared from view.

Amelia clenched her eyes shut. "God, don't let

her do something stupid 'cause she's mad with me." She stifled a sob.

Taking several deep, steadying breaths, Amelia retrieved her keys and locked the house. She was thankful Dad had picked Max up from school and put his apprentice-in-training grandson to work at the boat shop this afternoon. Waiting for her at church, they'd wonder at her delay.

Parking beside Dad's Silverado in the overflowing lot beside the sanctuary, Amelia hurried into the fellowship hall. On the menu tonight, Miss Jean's crab imperial and Miss Gloria's Smith Island cake. Enough said.

Amelia's mouth watered at the smells wafting from the church kitchen. Lunch in the cooler on the *Now I Sea* seemed like decades ago.

She spotted her dad running his mouth with the pastor, but couldn't locate Max in the sea of people crowding the newly refurbished fellowship hall. Until a familiar tropical-blue USCG uniform stood. A hesitant look in his brown eyes, Braeden twisted the cap in his hand.

Treacherous pleasure at the sight of him zinged through her veins.

Max peeked from behind the Guardsman's legs and waved. "Over here, Mimi!"

Heads turned and conversation died at the jet-engine decibel level of her beloved nephew's voice.

"What took you so long? Braeden and I been ready to eat forever."

Chuckles broke out across the room. Perspiration crept down the back of her neck. "Max!" she hissed. "Inside voice."

Braeden strode toward her with Max on his heels. "Hey, 'Melia. Fancy meeting you here." He cocked his head. "Long time no see."

He handed her a Chinet plate and gave her that lethal, one-sided grin of his. Amelia snatched the plate from his hand.

"Mimi," Max said, again with the not-so-inside voice. "It's not nice to—"

"I better see plenty of green beans on this plate, mister."

She thrust the plate at her nephew.

Max took the plate and raised his eyebrows at Braeden on the other side of the food-laden table. "Been ill all week, Brae."

She shuffled Max forward. "We're holding up the line." Not to mention creating a spectacle. "And I haven't been sick."

Braeden plopped a mound of coleslaw onto his plate.

"Not sick ill, Mimi." Max helped himself to three rolls. "Southern ill."

He leaned over the table in Braeden's direction. "Bad mood. Granddad says—"

"Max!"

Amelia fanned her face with her plate. Braeden

laughed out loud. As did several other ladies and gentlemen, including the mayor and choir director. Amelia propelled Max past the desserts and toward the eating area. She yanked out a chair.

"Sit." She pointed. "Plant your bottom in this chair. Don't you move until you eat every bite of your dinner and it's time for Awana."

Braeden positioned his plate across from Max. He smiled that crooked smile of his at her. Amelia's pulse went into overdrive.

She pivoted on her heel. "I'll get our drinks."

Braeden fell in alongside. "I'll help."

"Kind of hard not to move and chew at the same time, Meee-meee…"

Amelia cringed as Max's bellow followed her across the room. She stalked toward the ice tea glasses at the cutout kitchen window. Braeden eased in at her elbow as they waited their turn. His body shook with laughter.

She bristled. "Don't encourage him."

"I love that boy, 'Melia Duer." He slanted his eyes at her. "Love how he knows just the right buttons to push. He's so bright. Full of—"

"Max is full of something, all right. What're you doing here? I left your usual Wednesday-night plate in the microwave."

She reached for a plastic glass the same moment Braeden chose that one, too. Drawing back, she knocked over two adjacent cups. She gasped.

Ice cubes sloshed and sweet tea dribbled off the countertop.

Braeden grabbed for another cup to keep it from rolling off the edge. "Note my lightning-quick reflexes."

He batted his eyes at her. Way prettier than her own stubby, disappeared-without-mascara eyes.

Pauline Crockett, her former fiancé Jordan's mother, handed Amelia a stack of napkins. "Here. Let me grab a dishcloth."

Amelia closed her eyes.

God, take me now. Please. I'm begging You.

Braeden removed the napkins from Amelia's hand and proceeded to mop up the mess she'd—they'd—created.

"Where's your famous Shore—not to mention Christian—hospitality, Amelia Anne Duer? Don't you love how you've managed to wrangle this Coastie reprobate into these hallowed halls?"

Amelia opened her mouth to respond when Pauline sidled over with a dishcloth. She shoved the cloth at Amelia, and with a warm smile extended her hand to Braeden.

"Pauline Crockett, Mr. Scott. I'm so pleased to meet you after all the things I've heard."

Braeden gave Amelia a sidelong glance before shaking Pauline's hand. "Good things, I hope, Mrs. Crockett."

"Wasn't me." Amelia clamped her teeth together and scrubbed the counter. "Or it wouldn't be good."

Pauline's lips twitched. She exchanged the cloth in Amelia's hand for another tea glass. "Strawberries are at their peak this week, Amelia. Missed you last year."

Amelia clutched the cup as if her life depended on it. "I don't know if I can make it this year. Lots of charters scheduled."

She threw a look over her shoulder to make sure Max was okay. Her dad had taken a spot next to the small boy. Max also chatted with a fellow dinosaur enthusiast from Sunday school, probably attempting to offload—per Amelia's instructions—yet another Labrador pup.

"Your dad loves the strawberry jam you and Honey make. And Max loves the strawberry syrup with his pancakes. Your supply's bound to be getting low. To paraphrase an old song, you've got to gather those berries while you may. In May."

"I'm sorry for…for not…" Hot tears prickled Amelia's eyelids. "I—I don't know if I can, Pauline." She chewed at her lower lip. "Too late in the season. Maybe never…"

Braeden stilled. He placed a hand at the small of her back.

Pauline's gaze hopscotched between Amelia and the Guardsman. Her blue eyes softened. "The crops have been good this year. The sweetest strawberries I've seen in a long while, darlin'."

Amelia quivered.

Braeden took the drinks from Amelia.

"Please, Amelia? Try." Pauline leaned across the counter and squeezed her hand. "Friday?"

Amelia swallowed and nodded.

Pauline patted Amelia's arm. "Be sure you bring your little boy. And this big guy, too." She flashed Braeden a smile. "You know how I love a Coastie."

Amelia fought against the suffocating anguish with which she'd awoken each dawn since Jordan's death.

"Lots of buckets to fill, darlin'." She touched Amelia's cheek. "No worries. God is good. You're still in plenty of time."

Chapter Eleven

Outside the sanctuary, Braeden watched Amelia buckle Max into Seth's truck after the prayer meeting. Seth had promised a drive-by at the McDonald's in Onley for a milk shake if Max successfully completed his Bible memorization project this week.

Reverend Parks had spoken on a passage from Luke 5 in which Jesus told His fisherman followers to launch out into the deep, where not only provision awaited, but also an overflow of God's blessings. Recognizing a spiritual nudge, Braeden decided to reacquaint himself with the story when he got home.

Amelia waved to Max as Seth steered out of the parking lot. Swiveling toward the church, she gave Braeden a shy smile.

The breath whooshed out of Braeden's lungs.

He strolled over to Amelia and her Jeep. The now-familiar Pointer Sisters song came out of the cell tucked in the back pocket of her jeans.

Braeden smirked.

She rolled her eyes and fished it out. "Been meaning to change that, but—" Her eyes scanned the text message.

"What's wrong?"

She dug for the keys in her front pocket. The color drained from her face.

He snagged her wrist. "Amelia?"

She shrugged him off and scrambled inside the Jeep. "It's Honey. She's—"

The keys tumbled from her hand and clattered onto the asphalt.

Amelia laid her head on the steering wheel. "I begged her. I told her not to…"

Braeden retrieved the keys. "What's happened? Is she okay?"

She raised her head. "She's stranded at the beach in Ocean City." Amelia closed her eyes. "Oh, Honey. What have you done?"

"I'll drive you there."

Her eyes flew to his face. "No!" Her features shadowed. "I'm not sure in what state I'll find her."

Braeden tightened his jaw. "Kole's responsible for this, I'm guessing. Right?"

She gulped and nodded.

He squared his shoulders. "You're upset and there's no way I'm letting you go by yourself. Besides, I have a few choice words for my junior Guardsman."

"Kole's not there." She shook her head. "He

skipped out on her. Abandoned her. Left her all alone…"

"All the more reason why I should go."

Her eyes teared. "If anyone hears about this…" She gave a short, bitter laugh. "Who am I kidding? You flush a toilet at one end of the peninsula and seconds later everybody knows at the other end."

Amelia hit the wheel with the palm of her hand. "Stupid. Stupid. Stupid."

"Scoot over. You're in no shape to drive." He folded his arms. "I'm not letting you deal with this by yourself, 'Melia."

Amelia searched his face. Something she saw there apparently satisfied her.

"Okay. But I'd prefer you follow me in your own truck."

Braeden released the breath he hadn't realized he'd been holding. Waiting for her to trust him. Just a little. He raked a hand over his close-cropped hair. "I'll follow, Amelia. You lead. But wait for me before you search the beach."

He dogged her taillights for the almost ninety-minute drive north. Amelia wheeled onto US-113, headed east on Ocean Gateway over the bridge and zigzagged past boats docked at the marina. She drove past a thriving nightlife and steered toward a shabbier section of the waterfront.

Braeden pulled his truck into a well-lit convenience store parking lot across the street from the public access to the beach. Amelia steered the Jeep into the parking lot underneath an electric light next to the wooden steps. Honey sat huddled on the landing that straddled the dunes. Her back to them, she gazed out toward the dark, foaming waters of the ocean.

He threw open his door and slung his feet to the ground. A nearby engine turned over. A low-slung vehicle emerged from the shadows and edged past the corner of the store. His brow scrunched. The flashy blue Chevy merged into traffic and swung into a much-frequented watering hole farther down the boardwalk.

Traversing the two-lane road, he'd barely reached Amelia's Jeep before she launched herself out of the driver's side and barreled toward the steps.

"Amelia…" He grabbed her arm. "Hang on a sec. Let me take point on this."

She bit her lip but stepped aside.

Braeden glanced around the deserted beach and assessed the situation. He climbed the steps toward the platform.

Amelia hustled past him. "Honey…"

Honey burst into tears and covered her face with her hands. Amelia closed the distance separating them.

With a hiccuping, little girl-like sob, she stumbled into her sister's outstretched arms. "You were r-right. I should've never trusted h-him."

Amelia enfolded her into an embrace.

"Did Kole hurt you, Honey?" Braeden struggled to contain his fear and rage.

Honey's head shot up. She backed out of Amelia's arms. "No. He never once... We never..." Honey glared. "We always just sat in his car and talked. Or walked on the beach under the stars. Sawyer was always a perfect gentleman."

"Some gentleman." Amelia's mouth hardened. "Seeing how he abandoned you at night in a not-so-desirable part of town."

"I just don't understand what happened." Honey's face crumpled. "Yesterday everything between us was fine. I even told him—" she turned her face away "—that...that I loved him."

Amelia drew her close again.

Honey shook her head as if she couldn't quite bring herself to believe it. "All evening, it was as if he was trying to pick a fight with me. Then Sawyer brought me here. And he told me—" Honey's voice caught, but she straightened her spine. "Said I wasn't the kind of girl a guy like him wanted."

Braeden clenched his hands into fists.

Honey squeezed Amelia's arm. "Why? Why did he ruin everything?"

Braeden narrowed his eyes at Honey's choice of words. Honey rested her cheek on Amelia's shoulder, reminding Braeden of Max. "What's wrong with me?"

Amelia's face constricted. "Oh, sweetie, there's nothing wrong with you."

Braeden reached a hand toward them, but Amelia jerked away.

And anger stirred Braeden's gut. Yet another nail pounded in his Coastie courtship coffin thanks to Sawyer Kole. And not only with Amelia, but the whole Duer clan.

"Take her home, Amelia."

"What about—"

"My Coastie, my mess to clean up. Just get her home."

Defiance sparked from Amelia's stormy blue eyes, but a renewed round of sobbing prompted her to lead Honey toward the waiting Jeep.

Braeden navigated his truck toward the street and gunned it to the bar and his misguided coxswain.

The noise level hit Braeden before he even got out of his truck. The interior glowed neon. Similar Miami hot spots burned in Braeden's memories. And forestalled the swift retribution he'd like to impose on a particular young Guardsman.

He spotted Kole five spaces over, leaning against the hood of the Chevy. Clad in the same Western-cut shirt, jeans and boots he'd been wearing when Braeden last saw him at the station, Kole hunkered over an unopened beer.

Braeden sidled over. "Petty Officer Kole."

Sawyer's hand spasmed around the bottle.

"You're in a world of trouble, Boatswain's Mate."

Kole poked out his lips. "Like my record attests, nothing new." He gripped the alcoholic beverage.

Braeden adopted a nonchalant pose. "Because I know what's in your record from before you enlisted, I'd think twice about taking that first sip back to oblivion, Sawyer. Don't ruin your life."

Kole's hand shook.

"Your addict mother in and out of your life. Your father in prison after an alcohol-induced armed robbery. The foster homes. The hard work you put in to be different, to make something of yourself."

Kole kept his eyes fastened on the condensation etched across the glass bottle in his hand. "Maybe time to finally accept the inevitability of my gene pool."

Braeden crossed his arms. "I saw you parked beside the convenience store. You waited and watched to make sure she was okay until we arrived."

Kole hunched his shoulders.

"You cut her loose on purpose, didn't you, Sawyer?" Braeden sighed. "Don't know that I'd sanction your strategy, but your tactics were effective, albeit brutal."

Kole hurled the bottle toward a nearby Dumpster. Glass splintered against the sides and liquid spewed onto the sandy parking lot.

"Why'd you dump her tonight, Sawyer? Because she told you she—"

Kole reared. "Following your orders, XPO, not to ruin *her* life. 'Cause everyone who gets too close, I ruin."

"I'm sorry, Sawyer. I misjudged you." Braeden

scrutinized him. "You did this for her own good because you lov—"

Kole launched himself off the hood. "I don't love anyone. I can't afford to love anyone. Just the Guard. I got plans that don't involve this two-bit piece of land jutting into the Atlantic." His chest heaved.

Pity rose in Braeden's heart for the young man. A young man who uncomfortably reminded Braeden of himself after he'd lost his parents and Carly. "What can I do for you now, Kole? What do you need?"

Sawyer rocked back on his heels. "I need— I want to get off this peninsula. I can't face her again, Boats. I—" He swallowed. "I need an assignment with more action. Less time to think. More maritime enforcement potential."

Braeden nodded. "You'll get it, I promise, though USCG assignments don't exist for the Coastie, but the other way around." He shot the boy a look. "I've got a friend at headquarters..."

Sawyer widened his stance, his hands behind his back.

"I'll clear it with Chief Thomas. You can be on your way by daybreak."

Kole went into full military attention. He rammed the side of his hand into his forehead. "Thank you, Petty Officer Scott. But promise me, please—" His composure wavered. "Promise me you won't ever tell Honey the truth, or she might—"

"I don't believe in lying to people. Especially people I care about, Kole. But I will promise for now I'll keep this whole incident between you and me."

Later, when Braeden veered into the Duer driveway, he felt compelled to stop and check on Honey. And although apprehensive of his welcome, driven to check most particularly on Honey's older sister, who insisted on carrying everyone's pain on her own shoulders.

With the house lit like a Christmas tree, he found most of the Duers on the wraparound porch, backlit by the lights spilling from the interior. Ensconced in a rocker, Seth loaded his shotgun. His usually placid blue eyes glowed with a fierceness that gave Braeden pause. A human pogo stick, Max bounced from one end of the porch to the other. And Amelia shot Braeden a not-so-friendly look as his tread creaked on the steps.

She tugged at the box of cartridges in Seth's hand. "Daddy, please…"

"Why's Aunt Honey crying? What's wrong, Mimi? Are we going hunting, Granddad?"

"Lock and load. We're going huntin', all right, Max," Seth growled. "We're huntin' some here lowlifes tonight. Give 'em a taste of justice, Southernstyle."

"Daddy." Amelia rubbed her forehead. "Max, stop jumping." She flung out her hands. "Are you just going to stand there, Braeden, and let my father—"

"I took care of the situation, Mr. Duer."

"You did?" Amelia's voice squeaked. "What happened?"

Seth's eyes went to half-mast. Max stilled. Feigning a nonchalance he didn't feel, Braeden leaned against one of the railed columns. "Let's just say Sawyer Kole won't ever bother Honey again."

Seth grunted. "My daughter. Mine to protect. If I'd have known..." But he set down the gun and rubbed his grizzled chin.

"I know you would have, Mr. Duer. But part of my job is community relations and goodwill." Braeden grimaced. "Which, unfortunately, Kole single-handedly managed to sabotage tonight."

Amelia snatched the gun as Max inched closer, his eyes locked on the weapon. "Dad, you know better than to leave this lying about..."

Braeden grinned. Sounded like *aboot*. Amelia scowled at him and thrust the gun at Seth's chest. "Dad."

"Okay, okay. Simmer down." Seth patted Max's shoulder. "Couple more years, my boy, and I promise you we'll—"

"Dad!"

Seth laughed and the tension eased. He held out his hand to Braeden. After a second's hesitation, Braeden took it.

"Thanks for taking care of Honey." Seth cut his eyes at Amelia. "For taking care of both of my girls."

Amelia made a growling sound. Steam radiated off her like water evaporating on a July day in the Chesapeake.

"My pleasure, Mr. Duer."

Seth chuckled. "Still Seth to you, son." He slapped his gnarled hands upon the arms of the rocker. "Me and you, Maximillian, better go check on Honey." He shepherded a protesting Max toward the door and left Braeden alone on the porch with Amelia and her fury.

She advanced on his position with bloodlust in her eyes. "So what did you do to Kole?"

Not having been raised to be a fool, Braeden backpedaled a step.

"Bust his chops? Better yet, bust that arrogant, punk face of his. Smash his..." Amelia stalked closer. He retreated until his back pressed the railing. Sweet hospitality might drip from these Southern gals—until you got them good and riled. Then all bets were off.

He moistened his bottom lip. "I took care of it. Got him reassigned to another duty station off-Shore and far away. He'll be gone by morning."

"Oh." She uncoiled. "I guess I owe you my thanks, too." But just as quickly she repositioned the boulder-size chip on her shoulder. "Just another example of what happens when you let emotion overrule common sense with a Coastie."

His hopes sank to the depths of the Great Machipongo Inlet. "Amelia, let me explain what—"

She spun on her heel. "Not a mistake I intend to

make, I promise you." She yanked on the door handle. "I'm taking out a charter in a few short hours. Before daybreak. You can get your own breakfast."

"Aye, aye, Captain." Braeden gave her a mock salute. "Your gratitude is a little underwhelming, but in the Coast Guard, we live to serve, ma'am."

She slammed the door in his face.

His lips curved.

Don't call us, 'cause we won't call you, huh?

They'd just have to see about that. Because Shore Girl wasn't the only one as stubborn as a sea barnacle.

Chapter Twelve

First light dockside on Thursday, Braeden did not even try to keep the grin off his face at Amelia's startled look. He handed her a steaming mug of coffee.

She folded her arms against her You'll Love Our Nature, Eastern Shore, VA T-shirt. "What are you doing here?"

He planted his boat shoe against the *Now I Sea* railing. "Is that the only thing you can ever say to me, 'Melia? How about 'Good morning, Braeden'? How about showing me some of that lovable Eastern Shore nature?" He leaped aboard.

She scowled. "I'll show you some Eastern Shore nature..."

He grinned when she grabbed the sloshing mug from him.

"It's about balance, my dear Miss Duer. Like in life. Permission to board?"

She pursed her lips. "Looks as if you've already

boarded, Scott. Without my permission. But then again, you Coasties know about barging onto boats uninvited."

Braeden shaded his hand against his eyes as the sun topped the windswept dunes of the offshore barrier island. "Only for safety inspections. You're doing the work of two without a first mate on board." He pushed back his shoulders. "How's Honey doing?"

She coiled her fist around the handle of the ceramic mug. "Honey cried herself to sleep. She's not up yet." Her eyes narrowed. "Are you citing me, Scott? And last time I checked, a first mate wasn't a requirement for this size vessel."

Amelia held her other hand in the air, ticking off each finger. "I've filed a float plan with the marina harbormaster, got life jackets for each passenger, have a radio to contact help in case of an emergency and I carry signal flares in case I need rescue." She jutted her jaw. "And I repeat, I don't need a rescue."

He made a palms-up gesture. "Never would I presume to rescue a seasoned mariner such as yourself." Braeden reached for the bait bucket on the Duer dock. "And do I look as if I've come in an official capacity?"

Setting the bucket on deck, he angled to find Amelia's sea-blue eyes looking at him. She blushed and trained her gaze on the outgoing tide. "What have you come for, then?"

"Got a couple off duty days and I've come to offer my services as your first mate, that's what."

She pressed the coffee mug against her chest. "I didn't ask for your help."

He widened his stance, hands pressed behind his back. "I offered. Am offering. You've got customers waiting at the Kiptohanock dock and unless—" he cut his eyes left and right "—you plan to physically hoist me overboard, I don't see how you're going to stop me."

She mumbled something, probably uncomplimentary, under her breath. But she stepped aside.

Crossing his arms, he relaxed against the railing. "Good. I'm glad we understand each other."

She put her lips against the rim of the mug and took a deep drink.

Not trusting herself to speak?

Braeden smiled. "Red sky last night. It's going to be a gorgeous day."

And it was.

They chugged into the harbor and collected their six-person tour before 7:00 a.m. Amelia, tight-lipped, permitted him to welcome their guests on board.

Braeden made sure all the kids under thirteen donned life jackets. And he also spent a fair amount of time explaining safe boating rules. Once underway, Braeden busied himself demonstrating how to bait and hook the reels for these first-time deep-water fishermen. Skirting the tidal marshes, the

Now I Sea wove its way past the ruins of barrier island villages. Amelia gave an overview of once-thriving Eastern Shore fishing and farming communities that were now desolate coastal towns.

"The Blizzard of 1887." She steered away from Hog Island. "Nor'easter of 1910." Which she pronounced *noth'easter*.

One hand on the wheel, Amelia pointed to the stone foundations of a lighthouse on a smaller island not far, Braeden realized, from her Kiptohanock home.

"My Duer ancestors lived there back in the day. And before the modern Coast Guard, it was also the home of a lifesaving boat station until the hurricane of 1933 engulfed the island. A third of the island disappeared beneath the waves. Residents fled to the mainland, never to return. The ocean rises six inches every century. The islands shift, grow and shrink according to the whim of the tide."

She flicked him a look as if laying down a gauntlet.

Which he couldn't resist accepting.

"Tough Eastern Shore stock, the Duers. Survivors like my own hardy Alaskan forebears." Braeden gave her a crooked smile. "What a great gene pool we have between the two of us, Amelia."

She gave him a nice view of her back.

Clearing the last of the barrier island chain, she dropped anchor at a prime fishing spot a few miles offshore. The day was beautiful. The sun glinted off the ocean like a string of gemstones.

He shared tales of some of the more haphazard boaters he'd encountered in his years with the Guard, which sent the teenage guests into gales of laughter. One of the women allowed him the honor of setting her bait. Amelia shot the woman a disgruntled look after the fifth such time.

Around noon, Amelia moored in the crescent-moon bay near one of the deserted islands. Leaving the passengers to the lunches they'd brought on board, she grabbed her cooler and headed for the stern. Following in her wake, Braeden eased down beside her.

She scooted to make room and handed him a sandwich.

"Thanks. I hope I'm not robbing you of your well-deserved lunch."

She unwrapped another sandwich. "I always bring extra in case someone forgets to pack a lunch."

They chewed in silence for a moment. Shoulder to shoulder, they watched the seagulls wheel above them. Shorebirds hoping for a morsel of the bounty. Like him?

He smirked.

She cut her eyes at him. "What?"

"Nothing." Braeden took in a quick lungful of the fragrant sea air. "Quite the life you've carved out for yourself here. Peaceful. I can see why you love it."

She extended a bottle of water to him. "You do a great job pleasing the customers."

Braeden unscrewed the cap and took a big swig. He wiped his mouth with the back of his hand. "Only person I care about pleasing is the captain of this vessel."

Her cheeks rosied, but she stared him down. "Why do you care?"

"I thought we were friends." His voice, despite a determined effort, held a note of hurt. "Friends help each other. Has something changed that I'm not aware of?"

Amelia turned away, folding and squaring the brim of her Nandua Warrior ball cap. She said nothing, but gazed out over the breaking waves.

Her silence irritated him. Braeden frowned. "Isn't that the agreement we made? Until Max's all-clear report. Happy summer memories. Fourth of July picnic."

So not the whole truth. But Braeden was suddenly scared of what the truth might be. Scared of his feelings. Scared of what Amelia felt—or didn't feel—for him.

He ran his hand over his head, forgetting about his cap and sending it spiraling toward the water. Amelia made a quick grab for it. Braeden retrieved it from her with a sheepish grin. "Sorry. I seem to make a habit of losing my headgear, don't I?"

The real danger, if he was honest, was the danger

of losing his heart. Over one particular strawberry blonde Shore girl.

Braeden grimaced. He'd known she was trouble the moment he'd laid eyes on her. As if that fore-knowledge had done him any good in the long run.

Her lips quirked as if she read his thoughts. Braeden gulped. Sometimes he wondered if she could read him better than anyone he'd ever known. And yet, despite a well-earned caution, he couldn't seem to help himself. Couldn't stop seeking Amelia out. Searching for ways to be near her. To—

"How are Max's swim lessons going?"

Braeden cleared his throat. "He's a fish now."

She smiled and sipped her bottle of water. "He looks stronger every day. I'm so proud of him."

Braeden nodded. "We've progressed beyond the dog paddle to basic strokes. I got him to jump off the side yesterday." His mouth curved. "Max im-mediately wanted to try the diving board." Amelia gasped. "No worries. I told him one daredevil stunt at a time. His underwater mission tomorrow is to retrieve a coin off the bottom of the pool."

Her eyes rounded. "Really? He's come that far?"

Braeden tweaked the brim of her cap. "The kid has the heart of a true warrior. Like his aunt. No fear."

She sighed. "His aunt has a lot of fears."

Braeden laced his fingers through hers. And was inordinately pleased when she kept her hand in his. He brushed his thumb over the suntanned skin on her hand. "Maybe a better word is *courage*. That's what they teach us in the Guard. True courage moves forward despite the fear."

She raised her eyes from their entwined hands to his face. Never breaking eye contact, he lifted her hand to his lips. "Like you do, Amelia, every day."

Amelia worried her lower lip with her teeth.

"Tomorrow," she whispered. "Early half-day charter. Max has a teacher workday, and if you've got time, I could go with you and Max for the next lesson."

"I've always got time for you. And Max, Shore Girl."

"Oh, Braeden." She released a sigh so deep his heart pinged. "What am I going to do with you?"

Braeden held his breath as if with her answer, she balanced his entire life in her hands.

"How do you feel about picking strawberries afterward?" Amelia's voice sounded on the verge of tears. "I love strawberries."

Braeden's eyes locked onto hers. "Me, too." He tilted his head toward Amelia.

"Captain Duer? First Mate Scott? Is that a pod of dolphins starboard?"

She snatched her hand free and scrambled to her feet. "Where?" She headed toward her clients lounging at the bow of the boat.

And the moment passed.

For now, Braeden promised himself. Just for now.

* * *

"Are you going to die, too, Braeden?" Max jerked his head toward the white clapboard farmhouse. "Like him?"

"Like who, Max?" Braeden shook his head. "No, I'm not planning on dying anytime soon. But God's the one in charge of that, not me."

Braeden's eyes widened. Had he—Braeden Patrick Scott—actually just said that?

"Like Miss Pauline's son, Jordan. He and Mimi were friends. They were s'posed to get married."

Braeden swallowed. Max dangled his legs off the tailgate and let them swing. "He died when I went to the hospital across the bay the first time. Granddad crossed the bridge to tell Mimi."

"He was Coast Guard?" Braeden darted a glance at the house into which Amelia had disappeared.

Max nodded. "That's the saddest I ever saw her."

Braeden's gut clenched. Amelia's "friend" had died in the line of duty? He recalled the angry words Honey had hurled at her sister a few weeks earlier.

The little boy pumped his legs scissor-like, as if treading water. "Thing is, when I die—"

"Max." Braeden laid his hand on top of Max's shins to stop him and gain the boy's attention. "You're not going to die."

The boy shrugged. "I don't want Mimi to be alone. And sad." Max peered at him. "You make her laugh. She likes you. I can tell."

Braeden captured Max's small hand. "You're not going to die."

Max curled his fingers through Braeden's. "I'm not scared. Mimi 'splained it to me when it hurt real bad last time. She says dying's like pushing off into the water from the shore." He squeezed Braeden's hand. "Or like letting go of the side of the pool, I figure. The hard part in dying, Mimi says, is letting go of what you know."

Braeden's heart seized.

Max motioned to the ribbon of water visible through the trees. "But you got to let go and push out toward deeper water." Max smiled. "Mimi says not to be afraid. The best stuff, the biggest fish, are always found in the deeper water."

The screen door banged against the door frame. Amelia, in her faded jeans and hole-in-the-big-toe hot pink Keds, strode across the lawn toward them. She gripped several white plastic buckets. His pulse quickened.

Max smacked his lips. "I bet I can fill my bucket quicker than a Coastie." He propelled himself off the tailgate and raced to meet his aunt halfway.

Braeden focused on Amelia. Her eyes were red rimmed, as if she'd been crying. She sniffed and pulled herself together once Max drew closer. She laughed at something Max said.

Catching sight of Braeden, a pinpoint of light warmed her eyes. And a tiny smile, for him, lifted one corner of her mouth.

He yearned to touch the fiery sunlight of her hair. To hold her in the circle of his arms. She held one of the buckets out to him. His heart beat double time.

Today called for full disclosure. A transparent vulnerability. Not only had Braeden sought the wrong answers to his life, but until now he'd been asking all the wrong questions.

Braeden squared his shoulders. *Either fish or cut bait, Scott. Sink or swim.*

Time to go deep.

Chapter Thirteen

"We're supposed to pay by the pound picked." Amelia laughed. "Maybe it'd be simpler to put Max on the scale."

Max squatted beside a cluster of ripened strawberry plants. He'd discarded his bucket two rows earlier. Now, as the red juice splattered over his cheeks testified, he was just feeding his face.

Reclining against the arching pecan tree, Amelia jostled the lounging Coastie. "And he's not the only one."

Braeden gestured toward the buckets overflowing with red berries. "I picked my weight in strawberries, I'll have you know." He leaned on his elbow, propping his head in his hand.

His gaze roamed across her face. The warmth in his regard took Amelia's breath. Blushing at the intensity in his eyes, she focused on the muscle jumping in his jaw.

What was happening here? To her common sense? To her heart?

She'd do well to remember Lindi and now Honey—and the pain that followed such brief moments of bliss. She had responsibilities. No time for such nonsense.

Max. Her father. The boat. Obligations...

She closed her eyes against a rush of feeling. Willed the beating of her heart to slow. She opened her eyes to find his gaze still fixed on her. And imagined what it would be like to kiss Braeden Scott. To be cared for by a man who seemed determined to undermine her previous notions of love and the Guard.

Addled by his nearness, Amelia scrambled to a sitting position, scraping against the bark. Had she completely lost what was left of her mind? First Petty Officer Scott was, if nothing else, way out of her league when it came to matters of the heart.

He'd already admitted to a broken engagement. This thing between them—chemistry or boredom? A master tease and flirt, it was probably his way of whiling away a late-spring afternoon.

Amelia cut her eyes at him, inordinately pleased to note a pulse continued to throb in his neck as he stared out over the strawberry fields.

He took a deep breath. "Shorin' up the barricades again, 'Melia?" Braeden searched her face for answers she couldn't give him. Answers she didn't know.

Amelia drew her legs to her chin. She nuzzled her cheek against the frayed jean patches covering her knees.

He frowned. "Not sure what I need to do or say to get you to trust me. To show you how much I care about you." Braeden combed his hand over his head. "'Cause I'm tired of being your friend."

She blinked. "What?"

Braeden nodded. "You heard me. You may choose to live in the land of self-delusion, but I won't." He grabbed her hand and laid it over his heart.

Her fingers splayed against his chest, she gasped as his heart hammered a beat to match her own.

Braeden's eyes blazed. "Feel my heartbeat, Amelia Duer. This is what happens every time I see you, much less get near you. And don't you dare lie to my face and tell me I don't have the same effect on you."

She tried yanking her hand out of his grasp. "Arrogant much, Coastie?"

He held on. "Is that what you're telling me, then? No effect? Be honest with yourself and me. Should I back off because I disgust you? Annoy you?" Braeden relinquished her hand. "Say the word and I'll find alternate housing and get out of your life."

"No." Panic knifed through Amelia. "I—I don't want you to leave." She seized hold of his hand. "You don't disgust me." She wove her fingers in his. "Although you are annoying."

Braeden gave her a lopsided grin. "Thanks for the ringing endorsement, Duer." His smile dimmed.

"You don't want me to leave because you need the rent money? Or because of Max? 'Cause whatever there is or is not between you and me has nothing to do with Max. Max in my life is a nonnegotiable. I'm going to make a good Coastie out of him, remember?"

With a half laugh, she pillowed her face into her knees. "I don't want you to leave because of me," she whispered.

"Good."

Silence, except for the humming of the cicadas, thrummed between them.

"I want to explain about Carly."

Her head snapped up. "You don't need... You already—"

"Carly walked into my life when I was feeling especially alone." He reddened.

Amelia shifted, unsure she wanted to hear this. Actually, quite sure she didn't want to hear this.

"Carly and I were never a good fit. A Coastie wife has to learn to live with the absences when the cutter is out at sea. That's who I am. What I do. She said I loved the Guard and the sailboat more than her."

"Did you?"

Braeden glanced away. "Yeah, I did love them more than her." His gaze darted to Amelia. "Not exactly building trust in my potential as a suitor, am I, 'Melia?"

A *suitor.* The old-fashioned word found a home in Amelia's heart.

His face fell. "There are things concerning Carly I'm not proud of. She was right about me. I poured my wages into paying off my sailboat and none into her fantasy wedding plans. Either out too long on sea duty or when in port, too obsessed with my dream sailboat. Not really Carly's fault she drifted to someone who'd be there for her 24/7."

Braeden tore off a blade of grass and rolled it between his fingers. Strong hands, yet capable of great tenderness when dealing with Max. Hands that reminded her of another Guardsman, Jordan Crockett.

Her guilt rose anew. But she reminded herself of Pauline Crockett's—and God's—unconditional love and forgiveness.

She stilled the motion of his hand. "You're not the only person who's ever lived with regrets. I'm learning God is bigger than those if we entrust them to Him."

He probed her features. "Maybe my real problem with commitment has always been the riskiness of that sort of love. All consuming. After losing my parents, maybe that's why I've devoted myself to something safe like my boat and my career."

"An admitted control freak like me." She patted his cheek, enjoying the feel of his stubble against her palm. "Although what you do is hardly safe. The sea is never predictable."

"Neither is love. And much harder to control."

Braeden blew out a breath and gave her a shaky laugh. "Kind of like trusting God, too. But I'm working on it." He tweaked the tip of her nose. "So we've both got trust issues. Soul mates, huh?"

"I don't know if I'd go that far..."

His eyes glinted. "How far are you ready to go?"

She tilted her head, knowing he baited her. Just pushing buttons to see how she'd react. "Testing the water, Scott? How deep are you talking about?"

"Aboot." His lips quirked. "I love it when you go all Shore girl on me."

She sniffed. "Says Mr. Accent From Nowhere. I'll have you know we're a distinct cultural group and proud of it."

He laughed. "I'm learning to love your distinct culture and this place more and more every day."

Love... That scary word again.

Amelia's stomach knotted.

His eyes beckoned. "I've got another question for you."

"What did I get myself into?" Amelia covered her face with her hands.

Honey laughed and continued to decap the strawberries onto the newspaper spread out on the table of the screened porch. "Either tell me what happened this afternoon with Braeden or get back to work." Honey flicked a glance at the overflowing buckets of berries. "Did you two lose your minds when you picked all these berries?"

Amelia bit down on a ripened strawberry, then held the green cap aloft. "Decapitated enough for you?"

Honey rolled her eyes. "Well, that's one way to do it. But I think you're going to be sick if you intend to work through the bucket that way."

Amelia screwed her eyes shut and groaned. "I'm already sick. I can't believe I agreed."

Honey leaned forward over the pile of hulls. "Agreed to what?"

Amelia's eyes flew open. She gripped the paring knife and concentrated on slicing a berry. "Never mind."

Honey gave Amelia a wicked grin. "Don't hold back on my account. I want every juicy detail. Let me live vicariously, 'Melia."

"I've lost my mind." Amelia slumped. "He asked if I'd go with him to the Coastie auxiliary dance at the Yacht Club." She swallowed. "As his date."

Honey screamed and raced around the table. She heaved Amelia upward. Amelia's chair fell back with a bang. Grabbing Amelia around her torso, she bounced them both up and down.

"Amelia. Amelia. Amelia…" Honey squealed.

"H-H-Honey." Amelia's teeth rattled. Exhaling, Honey relaxed her hold.

"This is going to be a disaster," Amelia fumed. "What was I thinking? I'm more chicken-fried Tammy and Johnny's diner than trust-fund Yacht

Club." She sagged in Honey's arms. "I don't even own a dress."

Honey thrust Amelia to arm's length. Hand on her chin, Honey gave Amelia a studied appraisal. "Liner on the eyes. Color on the lips." Reaching behind Amelia's head, Honey tweaked her sister's ponytail. "Definitely needs work."

Amelia jerked. "Watch it."

"Something floaty. Fun. Flirty. Cut above the knee—"

"Hey." Amelia batted Honey's hand. "This is a mistake of maritime proportions." She cocked her head. "You go with him instead."

"Braeden asked you, not me." Honey fluttered her eyelashes. "Although speaking of trust-fund types, if you're determined to leave Braeden high and dry, I could always ask that snooty Onancock Robinson girl we went to high school with if she's available."

Amelia stiffened. "I think not."

Honey smirked. "That's right, 'Melia. Establish your territorial waters. He's *your* Prince Charming. Nobody else's." She corralled Amelia around the waist again and rocked her. "'Melia, 'Melia, 'Melia."

Amelia tugged free. "Don't go building fairy-tale schooners in the sky, sis." She held up her index finger. "I agreed to one date. One."

"Braeden is the picture in the dictionary beside *honorable* and *handsome*."

Amelia's head flopped onto her shoulders. "But I'm no Cinderella. And you know what happens at midnight." She swallowed past the knot in her throat. "Leastways, he'll never ask for another date. Not after I'm done humiliating myself and setting his career back a rating or two."

Ignoring her, Honey beamed. "It'll be so romantic. Dancing under the stars, kisses in the moonlight—"

"Gross."

The sisters stared at Max through the screen, where he stood pinching his nostrils together. Exchanging a look, the sisters giggled.

"Don't worry about a thing." Honey waved her hand. "Trust me."

Which only added to the coiled knot in Amelia's stomach.

"Remind me when this fancy shindig takes place?"

Amelia deflated. "One week from today."

Honey screamed. Amelia bolted upright. Max, both hands over his ears, yelled just because he could. Blackie howled from inside the kitchen. The remaining puppies, including Ajax, whimpered.

"Get your butt in here this instant, Max." Honey flung open the screen door. "Let me be the first to introduce you to how a strawberry huller works." She hustled Max into the chair she'd vacated. "You two—" Honey jabbed a finger Amelia's way "—have a lot of strawberries to turn into jam. And I've got a lot of phone calls to make."

Chapter Fourteen

Amelia headed out onto the open-channel waters at first light the next day, fearing her fingers were stained a permanent red after a long evening making freezer jam. With oceanside at the height of the flounder season, she spent the next few days running the boat in and out of the harbor and ferrying clients. Braeden was on the watch list, and she was without a first mate again.

Which she'd done just fine without until he showed up in her life, she reminded herself for the hundredth time.

But a charter without Braeden certainly made for a lonelier, less lively cruise. To make matters worse, Amelia had hidden her sketch pad from herself. Running late as usual, despite a quick, frantic search, she'd finally given up the quest as lost for now.

What really annoyed her, however, was seeing Braeden tying off *The Trouble with Redheads* at the

Duer dock when she returned at sunset. This time, a carrot-topped boy waved at her. On Sunday it had been Honey. On Saturday, her dad.

Everyone had been out on Braeden's sleek sailboat but her.

Knowing only one speed—full speed ahead—Max charged toward the house, probably in search of dinner. Amelia's heart felt empty and strangely neglected. Especially after all the time she and Braeden had spent together last week. Despite his declarations about exploring their relationship further, he'd kept busy—avoiding her? Doubt twisted Amelia's insides. Back to his true loves—the Guard and his boat? Amelia was starting to feel a great deal of kinship with the fickle-hearted Carly.

Therefore with no small measure of annoyance, she disdained Braeden's belated attempts at neighborliness and secured the mooring lines to the cleat on the dock by herself.

He grinned at her. "Catch anything today?"

She scowled. "Some."

Reaching over the side of the boat, Amelia offloaded the now empty bait buckets. Braeden relieved her of the buckets and set them down beside him on the dock. "Going to ask me about my day?"

She raised her lip. "Looks as if your day went well if you had time for a sail."

He chuckled, ignoring her waspish tone. "Yep. Finally getting around to exploring the inner passage. Don't know I want to venture out there in the dark, though. Too many hazards like sandbars and jetties. Lots of changeable inlets."

Braeden offered his hand to hoist her onto the dock. "Like some women I know, with their ever-changing moods."

She glared at him. "Did you call me moody?" She scorned his outstretched hand.

"If the Wellington fits."

She stamped said Wellington, which lost some of her intended effect by making a squelching sound on the deck boards.

"How about I help get your boat shipshape and tidy before tomorrow's charter?"

She gave him a snarky look. "How about you mind your own business and tend to your own boat?" Seizing the stanchion, she positioned one foot on the seat and placed the other on the rail.

A smile flickered across his face. "Why, Amelia. I've missed you this week, too."

In a sudden move, he plucked her around the waist and hauled her over the gap and onto the pier. Colliding with his chest, she made a sound not unlike the squawking of an angry seagull. He tightened his arms around her to prevent her from sprawling backward into the Machipongo drink.

"I ought to deck you, Scott..."

That infuriating, know-it-all grin. "Is that what you've really been wanting to do to me all week, Amelia?"

Telltale heat flushed from beneath Amelia's

T-shirt up her neck. That was the real trouble with being a redhead, she rued, not for the first time. Every thought shone crimson on her face, neck, chest and arms.

And a week without her sketch pad left way too much time on her hands to daydream...of him.

He laughed and pressed her closer.

Amelia's lips twisted. She hated being so easy to read. "I smell like fish."

His face alight, Braeden touched her dangling sea-glass earring and set it in motion. "You smell like the wind, salt and the sea." He inhaled. "My favorite smells in the world."

Amelia stilled.

Placing her palms against the blue cotton fabric of his shirt, she felt his heart stutter-step. Amelia wound her arms around his neck. Braeden lowered his mouth as she tilted her head. Her insides fluttered like a kite in a sea wind. Then their lips touched.

"A-meel-yaaa!"

She jerked. Braeden dropped his cheek against her neck and ground his teeth.

"A-meel-yaaa!"

"Thanks a lot, Honey," he growled.

Honey sprinted down the path toward them. And with a surge of fear and guilt, Amelia's next thought centered on Max. Before she could move, Honey's words sailed on the wind.

"The phone. Doctor. Lab results. Max."

Her heart plummeted to her toes. She gaped at Braeden. "What if—"

Mr. Always Ready broke the paralysis on her heart. "Go, 'Melia. Run. Trust, not fear."

She grabbed his hand. "Come on, then." And she dashed toward the house and the news that would—good or bad—change her life forever.

Perhaps Amelia allowing Braeden to be an integral part of the life-and-death drama playing out in the Duer family was the single most complimentary—and humbling—gift of his life.

"Where's Max?" Braeden whispered to Honey as they huddled in the doorway of the kitchen. Amelia crept to the landline phone like a soldier crawling out of a trench toward gunfire.

"He and Dad went to Be-Lo on a bread run for dinner."

Braeden nodded. "Probably a good thing."

Amelia stretched a shaky hand toward the phone lying on the counter where Honey had flung it. Her eyes darted to his. "Pray," she mouthed.

He swallowed past the boulder lodged in his throat. "I have been and continue to do so."

Something sweet welled in her eyes just for him. Then Amelia took a deep breath and snatched the phone. "Amelia Duer speaking."

Honey closed her eyes and folded her hands in prayer. Braeden couldn't take his eyes off Amelia, the bravest woman he'd ever known. Braver than any Guardsman in the face of the fiercest storm he'd ever seen.

Oh, God, I know it's been a long time since we were friends. But please...good news for Max. For Amelia.

"You're sure?"

He clenched his fists at his side, straining with the effort not to do something. Something only a God as big and great as the ocean He'd created could do.

"Absolutely positive?" Her voice had gone flat. "There's no possibility of a mistake?"

He stopped breathing.

"Thank you, Dr. Wallace," Amelia rasped. "For everything you've done."

He made a move toward her. Clutching the phone still pressed against her ear, her eyes widened at him. He froze.

Silence stretched as taut as a bowline.

"Amelia?" Honey whispered in a little-girl voice.

Mute, Amelia held the phone out to him. Hearing a dull dial tone, he switched off the phone. She staggered against the table.

Braeden caught her in his arms. "It's going to be okay, baby. Whatever the doctor said, we'll make it okay. God will make it okay, I promise."

He heard his own voice as if from a distance in an overwhelming need to comfort and console. "Into the deep with Max. Together. No matter what."

Amelia shook her head. Her eyes focused out the

window at the tidal creek. "His blood count is normal. We've reached the two-year mark. Remission."

Honey sank to her knees, laid her forehead on the floor and wailed.

Amelia gripped his upper arms. "Cancer-free. Chances after this long of moving out of remission are slim." Amelia shut her eyes. "He's not going to die. So much to be thankful for. So much to live for."

Braeden held her close. "So many summers to enjoy, Amelia."

She gazed into his eyes. "Sand dunes. Sunshine. Sea glass."

He nodded, his heart and soul full for the first time since he was a boy. "Fourth of July picnic, here we come."

When Seth and Max arrived home a few moments later, Max appeared dazed at the news, caught totally off guard. Braeden hoisted the little guy onto his shoulders. Amelia's, Honey's and Seth's arms enveloped each other. Braeden declared a party was in order.

"My treat." He grinned. "Where should we go to celebrate the best news ever, Max?"

Amelia pivoted. "Braeden, you don't—"

"Hush, woman." Braeden softened his words to Amelia with a smile. "This once."

She blushed. "Okay. The Wendy's or McDonald's in Onley?"

Braeden lowered Max to his feet. "*Please*, Amelia. I think I can do better than fast food."

He glanced from Honey to Seth. "How aboot—" Braeden flushed.

Seth chuckled and clapped Braeden on the back. "We'll make a real Eastern Shoreman out of you yet, son."

Braeden licked his lips to rephrase.

"How about—" Amelia smirked "—The Island House?"

Max tugged at his hand. "I want the chicken nuggets and fries at Tammy and Johnny's."

Braeden's eyebrows arched. "Really?"

Amelia laughed and knelt beside Max. She planted a kiss on his forehead before the wiggling boy broke free. "A man after my own heart."

She threw a look Braeden wasn't sure how to interpret in Honey's direction.

His gaze ping-ponged between the sisters. "Okay…" He blew out a breath. "Chicken-fried everything it is."

"Gotta get my little guy cleaned up first." Amelia hustled Max upstairs to change his shirt.

Seth stroked his mustache. "Guess a little spit and polish wouldn't do me any harm, either." He lumbered after his daughter and grandson.

"Ah, Honey…" Braeden bit his lip.

Honey halted on the verge of sailing out of the kitchen.

"I've been thinking about the Coastie dance thing."

Honey crossed her arms and rocked on her heels. "What about it?"

"Your dad told me that money's tight right now." Braeden drew a circle on the hardwood with the toe of his boat shoe. "But I wanted to make sure Amelia wasn't stressing over having something to wear." Braeden squared his shoulders. "I know better than to approach Little Miss Independence with this, but I want to give you some money to make sure she buys exactly what she wan—"

Honey threw her arms around his neck, almost knocking Braeden off his feet.

"Braeden Scott, you restore my faith in good men. 'Melia may not be ready to say it yet, but I absolutely adore you."

The breath whooshed out of him.

Honey patted his cheek and started for the stairs.

"The money," he whispered, with a pointed glance at the ceiling.

Honey smiled. "No worries, Coastie. I've got this under control. Amelia Anne Duer's going to take the wind right out of your sails come Friday night."

Braeden's heart jackhammered.

Because the truth was, Amelia Anne Duer—aka Shore Girl—already took the wind right out of his sails.

"Is this really necessary, Honey?"

Amelia clutched the salon chair armrests.

Honey made a piffling noise. "She won't need a tan, Wanda. Got about as much of a tan as redheads ever get anyway."

Amelia glared. "Hey."

"I'm thinking a French twist on the nape of her neck." Wanda tugged at the band holding Amelia's hair out of her face.

"Ouch."

Cindy made a face. "After you repair the number the sun, salt and wind have done to her hair first."

Amelia's brow furrowed. "I thought you were my friends."

Emilie patted her cheek. "We are your friends. That's why we've staged an intervention."

Amelia scrunched her nose as fumes rose from the concoction Wanda stirred in a bowl. She squirmed. "Seriously? You're not putting that in my hair, are you?"

Wanda snorted. "This isn't for your hair, sweet girl. This is for your face."

Amelia gasped and shrank back.

The overhead bell jingled as Debbie hurried into the beauty salon. She held up a Peebles bag. "Raided the cosmetics counter."

Amelia groaned. "Y'all know, turning this ugly duckling into a slightly less unattractive swan is a lost cause."

Honey huffed. "Amelia, stop being so negative. If you'd relax and make up your mind to enjoy the process…"

"Yeah." Cindy skewered her with a look. "It's the journey, not the destination."

Debbie nodded. "But when we get through with you, the destination is going to be fabulous, too."

Emilie rummaged through the cosmetics bag. "You won't recognize yourself."

Amelia screwed her eyes shut. "That's what I'm afraid of. Although…" Her eyes flew open. "Making me look like a girl instead of a grungy fisherman can only be a positive from Braeden's point of view."

Cindy lifted her chin. "Braeden's point of view of you must be fine if he asked you to this dance."

Amelia's stomach burned. "Probably a pity date for the old maid Duer sister."

The ladies shook their heads at each other. "What'd I tell you? Hopeless." Honey rolled her eyes. "This one's going to have to be pried kicking and screeching out of her trusty Wellingtons before we can get her into glass slippers, much less a tiara."

Amelia recoiled. "I'm absolutely not wearing a tiara."

"Only a metaphor, sis." Honey made an expansive gesture. "You see what I've been up against? This is exactly why I called in reinforcements. Speaking of which…?"

Everyone turned as the front door jingled again. Kathy cruised in holding a dry-cleaning bag aloft. "Miss Betty just finished the alterations."

Amelia quivered with both fear and anticipation. Which summed up her feelings regarding this dance and Braeden, too. Honey had taken her measurements and gone shopping without her.

Honey clapped her hands together. "Time for the big reveal."

With the plastic removed, Amelia's breath caught. "Oh, Honey..."

"Do you like it?" Honey chewed her lip. "If not, the New to Me shop will take it back even with the alterations. It's a brand-new designer dress. Tags still on it from the boutique on the strand in Chincoteague."

"And such a bargain secondhand." Emilie and the rest of the ladies gathered around.

Kathy adjusted a fold on the dress. "Some rich come-here woman probably decided to buy a new wardrobe for herself before ever wearing this one."

"It's beautiful." Amelia fingered the filmy, flouncy hem. "Honey, I don't know what to say."

Honey sniffed. "Nothing to say. Except you're going to have the time of your life tomorrow night." She grimaced. "Despite yourself."

Amelia sighed. "Good luck releasing this girl's inner Cinderella." She peered at her reflection in the mirror.

"But first things first." Amelia rubbed her index finger over the bridge of her nose. "You got anything in that bag of tricks to cover a few freckles?"

Chapter Fifteen

Pirouetting in front of the full-length mirror, Amelia's blue-green dress flared. Its filminess enveloped her body. The silky gathered hemline teased her kneecaps.

Fingering the soft spaghetti straps, she probed her reflection. "This looks nothing like the real me."

Honey stepped back, to examine the finished product. "You look fabulous."

Amelia sighed. "Exactly. Totally unlike the real me."

Honey pinched Amelia's upper arm. "Ow!" Amelia wrenched free.

"Some mascara and eyeliner. A little blush. Lip gloss. The real you underneath the Wellingtons, tank top and jeans simply waiting to be released. Think of it as a salvage operation."

Amelia wrinkled her nose. "Speaking of Wellingtons?" She stuck out one foot clad in a ridiculously high heel. "I'm going to break my neck trying to navigate the Yacht Club in these."

Honey tucked a runaway tendril behind Amelia's ear. "I told you to practice the stairs with them this week. To break them in."

"I've been kind of busy."

Honey sniffed. "Busy trying to avoid Braeden and put off the inevitable."

Amelia wobbled her head, feeling the weight of her locks pinned and sprayed into a neat bun on the top of her head. She missed her ponytail. "He's been avoiding me. Not the other way around."

Braeden had zoomed in and out of the property all day. Amelia knew this because she'd kept a surreptitious watch on the cabin, his truck and his activity.

She wandered to the window in the third-floor attic Honey had refurbished and claimed as her own. "He loaded the boat onto the trailer and hitched it to his truck. I haven't seen him since." Amelia wheeled. "Maybe he finally realized what a disaster this so-called date would be and abandoned ship. And me."

Honey shook her head. "Braeden isn't like that. And wipe that hopeful look off your face at the unlikely prospect he's deserted you. Like it or not, this is happening."

Amelia moaned.

Honey gestured from the window to the bed. "So practice walking, sis. Move."

Amelia stomped toward her. Honey gave her a look not unlike one she'd received from their mother once when she'd put worms in Lindi's lunchbox. The dress flounced, swaying behind her in a magnificent wake. Amelia stopped to admire the effect and teetered.

Honey steadied her. "Careful. Take it slow till you get used to the heels."

"The heels are the least of my worries." Amelia rotated her head on her shoulders, trying to iron out the kinks. "Who needs a facelift with a bun this tight? My head aches. I'm not sure I'm capable of blinking at this point."

She touched the nape of her neck and winced.

"Ever hear 'beauty is painful'? Well, it's true. Get used to it." Honey swatted her hand. "Quit fiddling with it. You're going to mess it up."

Amelia snorted. "Beauty and Amelia Anne Duer? A lost cause."

Honey's lips curved. "Not such a lost cause. I've seen the way Braeden looks at you when he thinks no one is watching."

Amelia's heart fluttered. "He watches me? Really?"

Honey tapped Amelia's silver lapis sea horse earring. "Really. And don't think I haven't spotted your lovesick glances his way, either."

"I'm not—"

"I want you to allow yourself the possibility of something more." Honey grasped Amelia's elbow and lugged her toward the window seat. "You deserve so much more."

Amelia sank onto the cushion and knotted her fingers in her lap. "I'm scared, Honey. I'm not like you or—"

Honey, none too gently, yanked Amelia's hands apart. "Stop comparing yourself to me or Lindi or anybody else." She cupped Amelia's cheek. "You were my lifeline when Mom died. Lindi's lifeline when she lay dying. Max's beloved Mimi when he got sick. Dad's anchor when his world washed away."

Tears trembled on the edges of Honey's lashes. "I love you, big sis. But this is your time, Amelia. Just for you. Don't let fear rob you of the joy God has for your life."

Amelia nodded, unable to trust herself to speak.

Honey brushed the moisture from underneath Amelia's eyes. "Don't cry. It'll ruin your mascara. And a redhead without mascara is—"

"A redhead without any eyes." Amelia swallowed the lump in her throat. She took a deep breath. "Okay. But I absolutely can't live with this tight do, Honey. Something's got to give." With a flick of her wrist, Amelia reached behind her head and pulled out the pins. Her hair cascaded around her shoulders.

Honey frowned. "Amel—"

"Girls!" Seth bellowed from downstairs.

Amelia cut her eyes at the alarm clock on Honey's nightstand. "Oh, no."

Honey rubbed her hands together. "Showtime. He's here."

Amelia shrank into the alcove, pressing her bare back against the cool pane of the glass. "I can't. I'm not ready."

Honey flung open the door to the stairs. "Get going, Duer. Move it."

Amelia glared at her sister. Honey drummed her fingers on her crossed arms. Amelia rose, chin tucked to her chest, and started her death march to the door.

"Oh, for the love of fried flounder..." Honey seized her arm and shoved Amelia onto the landing.

Catching hold of the banister, Amelia trained her eyes on descending each step. Overwhelming panic crushed her heart. She whirled to find Honey one step behind, blocking her only means of escape.

Honey pointed toward the second-story landing. "Go," she whispered.

On the landing, yet undetected, Amelia stalled. Her father and Max waited in the foyer below. Then Braeden, in full dress blues, stepped out of the shadows and into the light. Her throat constricted.

Wow. No surprise he cleaned up well. She rested her hand over her palpitating heart. Suppose he didn't like her dress? Or her hair? Suppose he didn't like her as much as she liked him?

But her foot lowered to the next step of its own

volition. As the stair creaked, Braeden's head snapped up. Her gaze locked onto his. Her heart lifted as his eyes warmed with appreciation.

Shivers skittered all the way down to Amelia's pink toenails.

Then she stumbled.

Braeden's heart stopped when Amelia emerged on the staircase. The gossamer dress mirrored the exact color of her beautiful blue-green eyes. His mouth went dry as her hair—for once free of her tomboy ponytail—swung free around her slim shoulders.

A funny little fear lanced his defenses.

So elegant. So unlike the Amelia who haunted his dreams with her cheeky grin, feisty Shore girl chip on her shoulder, who breathed sea, salt and wind.

Then she tottered. Her arms flailed. Braeden's eyes widened.

Amelia made a grab for the banister. Honey reached for her sister. He and Seth rushed forward.

But she caught herself. And grinned, embarrassed. Heat flooded her cheeks. And his mind eased. Underneath the glam, still his endearing Shore girl.

Braeden offered his hand. With a grateful smile, she entwined her hand into his. Braeden found himself uncharacteristically tongue-tied.

"Hey, Mimi." Max's eyes shone. "You look beautiful."

Seth kissed Amelia's cheek. "Yes, she does. All gussied up."

"Thank you, Dad." She gave them a tremulous smile. "And thank you, too, Max."

Max launched himself at Amelia's knees. She wrapped her arms around him and plopped a kiss on his carrot-topped head. "Careful, Max. I'm on stilts, and once I fall, I won't be able to get up."

He lifted his chin and snickered. "Like a beetle on its back?"

She arched her eyebrow. "Thanks, Max."

Honey joined them. "Max, get off Mimi. You're wrinkling her dress." She clasped Max's arm. "You're too big to be hanging on to Amelia like that."

"No." Max shook off Honey. "Don't leave me, Mimi." Burying his face in the folds of Amelia's dress, he clung tighter to her legs. "Where are you going, Mimi? I don't want Braeden to take you away."

Over his head, she exchanged puzzled looks with Braeden. Braeden crouched at Max's level. "You know where she's going, Max. I told you. Remember how you helped me get everything ready?"

Amelia's forehead creased. "Get what ready?"

"It's a secret." Max's voice deepened in an imitation, Braeden recognized with a grin, of his own. "A guys-only secret."

Amelia frowned. "Max, I don't like—"

"You're going to bring her back, though." Max's voice lost some of its assurance. "Right, Braeden?" He nestled his cheek against the silky fabric.

Braeden laid his hand on Max's shoulder. "Of course, Max. I promise. She's your Mimi forever. I'm only borrowing her tonight."

Amelia's hand drifted downward and covered Braeden's hand on Max's shoulder. "I'll be here when you wake up tomorrow, Max. Like always. Okay?"

"Okay... I love you, Mimi." Max sniffed her dress. "You smell good."

"Yes, she does." Braeden cleared his throat. "Like key lime pie. My favorite."

Amelia's eyes darted to Braeden's. A soft blush sculpted her cheeks as she bent once more over Max. She cradled his too-small body. "I love you, too, Max. You be a good boy and let Granddad and Aunt Honey put you to bed. No staying up late with Blackie."

Honey folded her arms. "No smuggling puppies into your bed, either."

"Aw..." Max scuffed the floor with his sneaker. "Please, Mimi. Just one?" He pursed his lips and raised his shoulder. "So I won't be lonely while you're on your playdate?"

She rounded her eyes at Braeden. "Playdate?"

Braeden grinned.

"Yeah." Max gave her legs one final squeeze. "Braeden said like when I go over to Dustin's."

Amelia cocked her head at Braeden. "We're going on a playdate like Dustin and Max, Petty Officer Scott?"

Seth and Honey laughed. It was Braeden's turn to redden. "Well…maybe not an exact analogy in our case." He stuffed his hands in his pockets.

An interesting expression flitted across Amelia's features. She gave Max a fierce kiss on the cheek before tickling his tummy. Giggling, Max let go and backed out of her reach.

"One puppy only in the bed." She held up her index finger. "One and no more."

Max nodded. "Scout's honor."

Amelia sighed. "Why doesn't that reassure me?"

Seth snorted. "Maybe 'cause he's not a Scout?" He hooked an arm around the boy's neck and towed him into a hug. "You kids go have fun. 'Bout time Max and I teach Honey how to fill the bait bucket."

Honey groaned.

Amelia cut her eyes at Braeden. "Time to fish or cut bait, huh?"

Pleasurable swirls of anticipation filled his belly. He extended his arm. "Shall we?"

Amelia saluted him. "Aye, aye, Coastie. Whatever you say."

He gave her a sidelong look. "I reserve the right to remind you later you said that."

Amelia threaded her arm through the crook of his elbow. "Well, then…let the playdate begin."

Chapter Sixteen

The setting sun cast a luminous glow over the Chesapeake Bay. And the Yacht Club blazed with hundreds of dazzling lights. Shimmering across the water, lanterns lined the pier behind the sprawling brick edifice. Festooned with twinkling lights, a flotilla of recreational motorboats and sailboats anchored inside the half-moon–shaped cove.

Sitting in Braeden's truck in the Yacht Club parking lot, Amelia put her hand over her heart, unable to believe her hardworking, no-fuss Shore world had been transformed into something out of a fairy tale. Which further served to remind her that she didn't belong here.

Braeden angled in the seat. "Wow."

She swallowed. "Spectacular, isn't it?"

"And the Club doesn't look too bad, either."

She lowered her eyes to her open-toed heels. "I'm sorry about Max earlier. I'm not sure what got into him. He's usually not so clingy. In fact, he's the child who pushes me away when I drop him off at Sunday school or kindergarten. Out of sight, out of mind."

"With you, Amelia, it's never a case of out of sight, out of mind. Not with me. Fact is, I haven't been able to get you out of my mind since a certain harpoon incident. The boy feels the momentousness of the occasion."

Amelia looked away, transfixed by the rapidly filling parking lot. "It's one night."

"It's as much as you want it to be, Amelia."

She bit her lip. "I'm not sure I can afford to believe in more, Braeden. Not sure I can risk—"

"Trust me, Amelia." He edged across the seat. She quieted as an aroma of sandalwood floated across the truck cab. "Look at me, Amelia."

She faced him and drank in the alluring scent of him. Braeden pushed back a strand of her hair with his fingers. His lips parted in a sigh.

Amelia's heart raced. *Breathe...*

Braeden's dark eyes pinned her. "You *are* beautiful. And strong. And fierce. And—"

Her throat caught. *Must remember to breathe...*

A burst of laughter from another pair of partygoers headed into the club broke the moment.

He raked a hand across his hair and heaved a deep breath. "What happened to your freckles, Shore Girl?"

She tossed her hair. "I thought you despised freckles."

He gave her a lopsided grin. "Not on you I don't. But never fear—" he gestured toward the clubhouse "—a Coastie is nothing if not prepared for every contingency. I've got a plan."

And before Amelia could fathom that mysterious announcement, he planted a quick kiss on her lips. "Strawberry. My favorite."

Her pulse skyrocketing, she gave him a sidelong look. "So you keep telling me." Amelia clutched the beaded purse Honey had insisted she carry. "What sort of plan? What have you and Max cooked up?"

"Stay right there." He gathered his headgear off the console and thrust his door open. Braeden positioned the hat and adjusted the brim. Striding around the truck, he threw open the passenger door and offered Amelia his arm. "Have a little faith, 'Melia."

She swung her feet to the ground and stepped out. He gave her a boyish grin as she twined her arm through his. He pressed her closer, the muscles strong and solid beneath her hand.

"Time to seize the day." He flicked a glance toward the anchored boats. "Or the evening." Braeden squeezed her hand. "Relax. You're going to have fun, I promise."

As he led her toward the throng gathered inside, Amelia prayed she wouldn't fall flat on her face and embarrass him.

Braeden held her arm in a tight grip as if he feared she'd give in to her instincts and make a run for it. Checking his hat at the door, he introduced her to several Guardsmen stationed at nearby Station Cape Charles whom he'd met while stationed long ago in Kodiak.

She managed to laugh in all the right places as the men shared glimpses of a younger Braeden Scott, brasher, less cocksure. And as they recalled his outrageous off duty exploits.

Braeden snagged two glasses of sparkling water off a passing waiter's tray. "Don't believe everything these Coasties tell you."

She batted her lashes at him. "I learned a long time ago I'd better not believe half of what a Coastie says." Braeden grimaced. "Although in your case..." She took her glass from him. "I'll bet they didn't tell the half of it."

The men laughed.

"Should have known better than to let you chat with my so-called friends." Braeden took her arm as the orchestra tuned. "I'm getting you away from here before these guys totally ruin my reputation."

The executive petty officer at Station Cape Charles grinned. "What reputation?"

"Ruin it with the truth, Scott?" Chief Thomas and his wife joined them.

Braeden's shoulders slumped. "You're killing me here."

Amelia set down her glass and laughed. "The truth hurts."

He drew her toward the parquet dance floor.

"Let's dance." She waggled her fingers goodbye at the men and the Thomases. The orchestra began a slow ballad.

"You gonna let me lead, Duer? Or am I going to have to fight you for the privilege of letting my friends see the prettiest girl in the room in my arms?"

"If I didn't know better, I'd swear you were Irish, spouting all sorts of blarney." She gave him a flirtatious look. "But I've got to warn you, I've never had much opportunity to dance."

"All you have to do is follow my lead." He encircled his hands around her waist. "Think you can handle that?"

Her arms drifted up to his shoulders. "I can follow anywhere you lead."

Braeden tightened his hold. "I'm not going to let you forget you said that."

She ran her gaze over the angular line of his jaw. "Of that, I'm sure."

After a few spins around the room, the tune changed to a faster cha-cha tempo. She tensed and Braeden released her. "Let's get something to eat before our next adventure."

"What next adventure?"

Again he smiled that Cheshire cat smile, which reminded her of Max. "Every day is an adventure since I met you, Amelia Duer." He tweaked her nose. "The night is young and further opportunities beckon. But first things first." He patted his stomach.

"Dare I ask what opportunities beckon tonight?"

He pried a glass plate off the buffet table and handed it to her. "Wait and be surprised."

She frowned. "I'm not real big on surprises, Scott."

"You'll enjoy this surprise, trust me."

Thing was, she did trust Braeden. Despite past experience, despite what her common sense told her to be true.

With their plates laden with lobster tails and soft-shell blue Chesapeake crab, they wended their way toward the glass-banked dining room overlooking the bay. Tables of eight topped with sea-green tablecloths and candlelight lent a flattering old-fashioned glow to the room. Conch shells and driftwood rounded out the centerpieces.

Chief Thomas waved them over. They settled beside him and his wife plus an assortment of retired Coasties, auxiliary volunteers and blue-blazered yacht patrons. After more introductions, the conversation shifted to speculation over the next Wallops Island space launch. Followed by a spirited debate over each man's golf handicap. And from there to the ladies' favorite five-star resorts around the world.

"Kinda out of my league—" Amelia leaned over for Braeden's ears only "—this bayside crowd. We oceanside folk work for a living."

His lips quirked. "Me, too. I grew up on a Bering Sea fishing boat, remember? But I've been out of my depth with you, Shore Girl, since we met."

She blushed to the roots of her hair. "Braeden..."

Braeden grinned, no trace of remorse. "Tonight, Amelia, I feel like the luckiest guy on earth."

Amelia, for tonight at least, felt as if she really was a princess. And Braeden Scott—a Coastie, of all things—truly was her Prince Charming.

Chapter Seventeen

"Keep your eyes closed. Trust me. I won't let you fall."

Amelia clung to his hand but kept her eyes squeezed shut. "Fall? Is that water I hear?"

"Open your eyes, 'Melia."

Her eyes flew open. "Your sailboat."

Braeden stepped over the gap between the boat and the Yacht Club pier to reach for her.

The corners of her mouth curved. "Is this your surprise?"

"Yep."

She took his hand, her slim, strong fingers cool against his. "You trailered your boat bayside at the Club?"

"Yep."

"Is that all you can say for yourself?" Amelia wobbled, trying to regain her balance in those ridiculous shoes.

"Here. Let me help." Braeden swept her into

his arms. She gasped but wound her arms tighter around his neck as he lifted her into the boat.

"Not the best shoes for a moonlight cruise, but Max and I prepared for the situation."

"A moonlight cruise?"

She felt good in his arms. Right. A sweet-scented breeze blew a strand of her hair across his face. His breath hitched.

"You can put me down now."

Light from the Yacht Club spilled across the water and illuminated her face.

"Yep." He grinned. "I could. Don't want to, though."

Snatches of music and laughter floated into the night. They contemplated each other. These were uncharted emotional waters for him. If she only knew what being close to her did to his heart.

He'd spent the past week searching his heart, praying on what he should do. Pondering what he could say to erode the last of the barriers with which she'd kept him at arm's length since they'd met. His feelings went beyond anything he'd ever experienced before.

And he—thanks to his rediscovered faith— wanted to show Amelia how much he respected, cherished and valued her.

Prayer—what a concept. Might have prevented him from making so many disastrous relationship choices since his dad died. But not this time, he promised himself. Not with someone as important to his life as Amelia.

With reluctance, he relinquished his hold upon her and helped her regain her footing on the deck. "And about those USCG regulations you love so much…"

He waited a heartbeat's space of time, anticipating her eye roll. And she didn't disappoint him. He grinned. "I'm adding one of my own while you're aboard this sailing vessel. Stay here."

Braeden hurried below deck to retrieve the duffel bag he'd stashed this afternoon. Returning, as his head topped the stairs, Braeden smiled at the sight of her puzzled face. Seated and waiting, as he'd instructed, where he left her.

Would wonders never cease.

Regaining the deck, he dropped to his knees at her feet. Her eyes rounded. "What are you doing?"

Braeden withdrew a pair of boat shoes from the bag. Her eyebrows rose. "Are those mine? Where did you—"

"Max." Braeden placed her foot on his knee.

She tucked the pleats of her dress around her body. "I can do it, Braeden. No need for you—" He ignored her and unstrapped the buckle. "Really. Let me—"

He eased her foot out of the high-heeled shoe. "No, let me do the honors, please." She tensed. He studied her. "Trust me, Amelia. Trust yourself."

She shivered, but she didn't break eye contact.

"I do trust you, Braeden. I'm not sure I should, but I do."

Amelia allowed him to guide her foot into the boat shoe. He lowered her foot and held out his hand, waiting.

His heart thudded.

She raised her other foot and placed it into his open palm. "Good thing Honey convinced me to paint my toenails. Or this might make me nervous."

He laughed, as she'd probably meant him to, breaking the tension of the moment. He fumbled with the strap. Finally he slipped her bare foot into the other shoe, eager to get this sail underway.

"There you go." He helped Amelia stand. "And because the wind across the water can get nippy when the sun goes down, Max thought you might also need this." He plucked a lacy shawl from the confines of the bag.

"Max thought, huh?"

Braeden shrugged. "I suggested. Honey caught Max going through your dresser drawers. She loaned you this for tonight." He draped the shawl around her shoulders.

She brushed her cheek against its woven softness. "Got the whole family in on it, didn't you?"

Braeden fanned her hair out from the confines of the shawl till it tumbled free, falling down her back. "I love your hair." He curled one strand around his index finger.

"Oh, really?" She gestured toward the bow of the boat. "What about *The Trouble with Redheads*?"

Braeden unwound the runaway curl from his finger. Slowly. "From where I'm standing, the only trouble with redheads is that they are so lovable."

"Humph."

But he could tell from her heightened color he'd pleased her. "But you distract me. Permission to cast off, Captain Duer?"

"By all means, Coxswain. Wouldn't want to hold up the adventure."

Grasping her hand, he led her to a safe spot, out of the way of the boom and close to the wheel. "We're in luck. It's a perfect night for a sail. Just enough wind. Not too choppy. No fog."

Removing the fenders from the side of the boat, Braeden brought the engine to life, edged from the slip and maintained a low speed. "*The Trouble with Redheads* is fully rigged and ready to sail."

"Kind of sounds like a Coastie, no?"

Braeden grinned before turning his attention to a careful scrutiny of the running lights of the other boats docked at the marina. Dodging the other recreational vessels, he chugged farther from shore. "We won't go far tonight," he shouted over the noise of the motor.

He gradually accelerated as he cleared several yachts at anchor in the harbor. Once clear, he cut the engine and hoisted the sail. Downward of the wind, he let the sails all out and allowed the boat to run toward the neck of the channel.

Still in sight of the Club harbor on the other side of the cove, he sheltered the boat in the lee of the wind. Protected by the land from the force of the waves and wind. The moon reflected a path of silver across the tides lapping at the darkened shore.

"You really love this boat. And I can see why." Amelia gazed out over the water. "It's a lovely spot, if it is bayside." She injected a teasing lilt to her voice.

"Oceanside." He arched a look over the wheel. "Like its inhabitants, it is too unpredictable, especially at night."

"You went to a lot of trouble for me."

"Come here." He held out his hand. "For you, nothing is too much trouble."

He escorted her to the bow, where he'd stowed several cushions. "Let's see if we can spot the Milky Way."

She eased down beside him, resting against the wall of the cabin. "May be too much moonlight to see the stars."

"I see stars every time I'm around you, Amelia."

Averting her eyes, she fingered the lace on the shawl. "You're very sweet. Gallant in an old-fashioned way. And very good for my ego."

He lifted her chin with his forefinger. "I wish you would see yourself the way I see you. Brave to a fault. Heroic. Courag—"

"I'm not brave or courageous." She shook her head. "I'm definitely not heroic."

"After giving up your dreams for Max and your dad and…" He took a breath. "Losing Jordan Crockett."

"How do you— Let me guess." Her lips flattened. "Max spilled his guts again." Amelia wrapped the ends of the shawl closer around her body. "You don't understand how it was."

Jealousy over a dead man knifed through Braeden. Her devotion and loyalty superseded death. A love and devotion Braeden had never received from any woman. A devotion, Braeden was honest enough to admit, he'd never deserved.

Till now? Was there room in Amelia's heart for one more Coastie? For him?

"I'd like to understand, Amelia." He held his breath and prayed. For them both.

She lifted her face to the moon and closed her eyes. And just when he feared he'd lost her, she whispered, "We knew each other forever. You never think anything will happen to someone who's twenty years old. So full of life. So sweet. So…"

At the catch in her voice, Braeden yearned to touch her hand, to hold her, to keep her somehow tethered to him. And at the same time to sever this cord that bound her in the past. But as she shrank into herself and into her memories, he dared do neither.

"Honey would say we were BFFs. Since we were

little kids. I was always more comfortable playing baseball with the guys than playing dolls with those crybaby girls." She laughed, a sound without mirth. "Some things never change."

"Some things don't have to change, Amelia." Braeden clenched his fist. "You don't have to be Lindi or Honey or Caroline. Amelia Anne Duer does just fine being herself in my book."

Amelia darted a glance at him. "Amelia Anne Duer is a coward, Braeden."

He made a motion of protest.

"It's true. You want to know the real reason I never left the Shore? The real reason I turned down the scholarship and lost my chance to develop my art?"

"You could never be a coward. After you stood by Honey and Lindi and—"

"Max is brave. Lindi was brave. The real reason I gave up the scholarship wasn't because Dad and Honey needed me when Mom died. The real reason I stay here, the real reason I took on Dad and Honey and Lindi and Max, is that I'm selfish."

He frowned. "Selfish? You don't have a selfish—"

"You pegged me the first time you laid eyes on me, Braeden. Fear. I was too scared to leave behind everything I'd ever known and loved to go to Savannah. Scared I'd never fit in. Scared of being lonely. Scared to leave my comfortable, safe Eastern Shore cradle. Every decision I've ever made has been based on fear. I'm scared to death."

She snorted. "I'm scared of life. I'm scared of failing, so I don't try. And therefore I automatically fail, because I'm too afraid to try."

Braeden seized her hand. "You're too hard on yourself. None of this is true. Not really."

Her face constricted. "He loved me, Braeden. Jordan loved me. The only one who has ever loved me that way. Who will ever—"

"No, that's not true, either. He's not the only one who will ever love you."

Startled, she blinked. "You don't know how I hurt him. Why I deserve to be alone."

Amelia took a deep breath, and continued.

"When he enlisted, he promised as soon as he received his first assignment, he'd send for me and we'd be married. I let him go off to boot camp knowing I had everything I'd ever need right here and that I'd never go off-Shore. Not even for him. Like you with your boat and Carly, I didn't love him enough. Not enough to go with him. And when he sent for me to come to Oregon, I refused."

Her mouth pulled downward. "I couldn't do it. I can't breathe when I'm not here. When I'm not out on the water. But I broke his heart, and two weeks later he died on a rescue mission."

"Amelia, I—"

"Don't say anything to me." She scrambled to her feet. "'Cause I'll only end up hurting you. Maybe endangering your life, too."

He rose and grasped her arms. "I'm willing to

take the chance, Amelia. I'm tougher than I look. Don't let this ruggedly handsome exterior fool you."

She slumped against his chest and choked back a half-sobbing laugh. "That ego of yours, Coastie, could charm fish out of the water."

"Only one fishergirl I'm interested in charming." He brought her hand to his lips. "Would you give me a chance to prove you wrong? Would you give us a chance? Yourself a chance for happiness?"

She shuddered with sobs held too long inside. "Baby steps?" she whispered.

"I'm not in a hurry. And I'm not going anywhere."

"You say that now."

"Amelia, look at me."

She raised her eyes to his. The pain in her face, the fear, the uncertainty stabbed at his chest. "Believe me. Faith, not fear. Trust in us."

Her lips trembled. Moisture quivered on her lashes. She shifted her gaze toward the stars, where pinpricks of light dotted the blue velvet curtain of the celestial sky.

Braeden peered at the remaining sliver of the moon. "The moon's gone behind a cloud."

Amelia stirred. "Enough for a kiss in the moonlight, though."

Braeden angled. His heart pounded at her expression.

True to form, she never failed to astonish him. On her tiptoes, she cupped both sides of his face. His hands encircled her waist. Her mouth found his lips and something pure and sweet quickened his heartbeat. Something deep in his soul recognized and responded to this love for which he'd aimlessly searched and not found—until now.

Until this moment in the moonlight. Anchored in a safe harbor on the Eastern Shore of Virginia.

Not in the bright lights of Miami. Nor the adrenaline-pounding action of a cutter off Kodiak. But here with this woman. With this beautiful Shore girl, he'd found what he'd longed for without even realizing it his whole life.

And Braeden knew that he loved her. Loved her enough to sacrifice everything he'd mistakenly given his heart to before. Loved her enough to do what it took to make sure there were more moments like this in the moonlight.

More hours in her presence. More summer days. Winter, autumn and spring, too—building a life of sand dunes, sunshine and sea glass.

Bending to her height, he relished the feel of her soft lips on his. And she returned his affection.

When they pulled apart, they stared at each other. In her half-lidded gaze, he saw the hope in her eyes fighting valiantly against the fear.

And for once, winning.

Patience, he reminded himself. Slow and steady would win her heart. *God, don't let me mess this up, please. Not this time. Not with her.*

Where would Amelia want to go from here?

She clung to the sleeves of his jacket as if she

might fall without his strength. He tightened his hold and steadied her. He waited for her to say something. Anything. Waited for her to pull back and run away again.

He tried to steel his heart for Amelia's standard one step forward, two steps back routine. Tried and failed as he waited for her to lower the boom on his foolish hopes and dreams.

"Well..." She blew out a breath.

He swallowed. "That all—" His voice was husky. "That all you got to say?"

Braeden felt her smile. She lifted her face to his. His heart hitched as her lips brushed over his cheek.

"Will this sailboat turn into a pumpkin at midnight?" She laughed. "Or have we time for one more kiss before you take Cinderella home?"

He captured her face in his hands. "There's always time for you," he whispered.

Chapter Eighteen

The next week was like a barely remembered dream for Amelia. Full of exquisite moments of joy. Full of laughter and further adventures crabbing with Max in the tidal marsh.

Full of happiness as she shared her favorite barrier island spots by the light of the moon with this Coastie who'd managed to steal her heart. Though it wasn't even Memorial Day yet, she, Braeden and Max made plans to return and celebrate the Fourth of July in a big way, Eastern Shore–style.

She thrilled to after-dinner evenings on the screened porch with Braeden watching the herons and gulls. Endured the satisfied glances between her father and Honey. The knowing smiles of her friends and neighbors around the village. Amelia overflowed with a happiness she'd believed forever out of her reach.

For the hinges of her rusty heart were swinging wide and giving way to Braeden's inexorable charm. She loved the way his eyes lit when she entered a room.

And that scared Amelia almost witless at how essential he'd become to her well-being.

Daily reminders of past failures led to twinges of doubt. Doubts about the foolishness of trusting her heart, trusting a Coastie and the prospect of an uncertain future. But she prayed. Oh, how she prayed.

Could she love him enough to leave the safe harbor of Kiptohanock and entrust her heart into Braeden's hands when and if the time came to make a choice?

Even contemplating such an outcome scared Amelia all the more. Because this time, her heart was telling Amelia maybe...

Maybe yes.

"Are you sure you want to do this, Braeden?"

Braeden settled into the scrolled-iron chair outside the Corner Bakery in Onancock. "I'm sure."

His father's childhood friend, Master Chief William Davis, propped his elbows on the table between them. "I know how much you love that boat."

Braeden lifted one shoulder and let it drop. "Not as much as I love Amelia Duer."

Davis shook his head. "This place has changed you. I can hardly believe this is the same Braeden Scott who poured his heart and soul, not to mention every paycheck, into *The Trouble with Redheads*."

Braeden smiled. "The trouble with this particular Eastern Shore redhead is that she's taken my heart. God's taken my soul. And there's no going back with either."

Davis reached across the table and gripped Braeden's hand. "You have no idea how delighted I am to hear about your rediscovered faith. Your mom and dad..." He cleared his throat. "Everything I hoped you'd find here in this community, just as I did some thirty-odd years ago."

Braeden cocked his head. "You? Here?"

Davis released Braeden's hand and sat back. "Station Kiptohanock was my first duty station. Taught this salty old dog some new tricks. I'd hoped you'd find faith and a new beginning to your life here, as well." He chuckled. "Didn't count on a redhead in the picture, too."

Braeden gestured down Main Street past the galleries, bank and shops. "You taken a good look at this place lately? Can't throw a rock and not hit one." His lips quirked. "I never stood a chance, and you know it."

Another reason he'd chosen the bakery in Onancock and not the diner in Kiptohanock to conduct this delicate bit of business.

"You sure you want to sell your boat to my nephew?"

"I'm sure. He offered me a fair price the last time I bunked at your place for your sixtieth birthday bash. Amelia's overwhelmed with medical bills for Max. The Duers are going to lose their boat. The boat is their livelihood. She works too hard as it is. No time for anything for herself. She needs breathing room. Time for her art. This money will give her a new start, a way to begin again."

The master chief studied him. "Have I told you how proud I am of the man you've become? The man I always knew you had hidden away inside. The man your parents would be so proud of."

Braeden dropped his eyes to the pavement. "You may not be so thrilled when I tell you the rest of my news."

Davis held up his hand. "Before you make any ill-advised declarations, let me hasten to remind you about the exam for warrant officer rating."

Braeden started to shake his head.

"With your unique skill set and experience, it wouldn't be long till you advance. You can apply for the warrant to lieutenant program and bypass officer candidate school."

Braeden stared at him.

Davis nodded. "Or attend officer candidate school if you'd prefer that route and graduate as an ensign. I've made sure District Five headquarters has kept its eye on your performance here at Station Kiptohanock. A command of your own someday is not out of your reach."

For a moment, the ghost of the buccaneer present in every Guardsman tore at Braeden's resolve. But something stronger than his ambition vied for his heart—a redheaded Shore girl and a family he'd believed forever lost to someone like him but now found.

"I—I can't, Master Chief. My enlistment's almost finished and I don't plan to reup."

Davis let loose an explosive breath. "Not after all your hard work. Everything you've learned. The training the Guard has poured into you. You can't disregard the potential God gave you."

Braeden swallowed past the lump of emotion clogging his throat. Davis had been more than a mentor. He'd been a surrogate father after Braeden's own father lost his life to the sea. In hindsight, Braeden now realized that Davis's faith, like a rudder, had nudged him on a course back to God.

Davis leaned forward. "If you and Amelia are truly meant to be, why can't she follow you to your next assignment like a good Coastie wife?"

Braeden frowned. "It's complicated, Master Chief. She won't—can't—leave here. And I refuse to ask her to make one more sacrifice."

"You love the Guard life, Braeden. I know you. You'll never be happy, nor, I suspect, would she, knowing you sacrificed your dreams for her."

"Sometimes dreams change." His gaze locked onto Davis. "Sometimes we trade something wonderful for something of greater value."

Davis sighed. "You're sure this girl's worth the sacrifice? Worth what this will cost you and your career? Don't be hasty in making such a life-altering decision, son. Think on this. Better yet, pray on this. You give me a call anytime and we can sort through the advancement options together."

"I won't change my mind. It's time to go all in or nothing."

A man unused to being told no, Davis tapped his fingers on his table. "I'll give my nephew a call. I expect he'll send you a bank draft right away. I can drive him over next weekend to take possession and he'll probably want to sail to his slip at Annapolis if the weather's good. But, Braeden, this conversation isn't over by a long shot."

Braeden thought it best to leave the issue alone for now. When he failed to reenlist, the master chief would be forced to accept his decision, like it or not. Braeden had always suspected there was a picture of an Alaska-toughened native beside the word *stubborn* in the dictionary. But Braeden was an Alaskan, too, and Davis no longer held the monopoly on determination.

A done deal.

No going back. No convincing the bank to extend their generous terms of repayment for even one more week. This time next week, the *Now I Sea* would belong to the Eastern Shore Bank of America.

She'd have to cancel the summer charters, not that those charters would've been enough to keep up the payments on the boat. And without the boat with which to eke out some semblance of a living, foreclosure on the house would commence by autumn. She'd best start looking for a job.

Maybe someone bayside would hire her on as first mate. The Duers were known Shorewide for their honesty, faith and hard work. But Dad's and Honey's paychecks wouldn't stretch far in this economy.

And Duers did not take handouts.

With a sinking feeling, Amelia grappled with the inescapable conclusion she might be forced to go off-Shore to find significant work. She didn't have many skills. She could do the work of any mariner, though. And if worse came to worst, she'd sign on to the crew of an international freighter.

If worse came to worst? Amelia scrubbed her eyes before pushing open the glass-fronted door of the bank. As if leaving the Shore wasn't already the worst possible consequence.

She emerged only to spot someone down the block who resembled a certain Coastie shaking hands with an older, distinguished gentleman outside the Corner Bakery. Despite the grave news from her mortgage lender, her heart gave an involuntary flip.

Amelia lifted her hand to wave. "Braed—"

But the Braeden lookalike, with the older man in tow, disappeared in the direction of the Onancock marina. Amelia blinked. Couldn't be. She'd thought Braeden was on watch today.

The older guy wasn't someone she recognized as

being from around here, either. And if he was in the mood for doughnuts and coffee, no way Braeden would travel to Onancock instead of visiting the Sandpiper for their famous long johns.

She smiled at the memory of Braeden's first encounter with a long john. And her lips twitched as she recalled their first encounter—hers and Braeden's—with each other. A lot of water under that bridge.

Had it been only six weeks ago? Seemed as if they'd known each other forever. Amelia dropped her hand to her side.

She was so silly. So completely resembling every love-struck, doe-eyed woman she'd ever mocked, imagining the object of her affections on every street corner.

Get a grip, Shore Girl. That was what the executive petty officer would've told her.

She cut her eyes to see if anyone else had witnessed her making a fool out of herself. The coast appeared clear until Victor Kellam poked his head out of the Tidewater Galleria next door to the bank.

"Amelia Duer."

She halted midstride in front of the Mason-Davis Realty office. Perhaps if she appeared to be studying the cute bungalow listings taped to the front window, Victor would go away. She loved her childhood home, but how sweet some of these homes for sale would be.

"A-meel-yaaa…"

She focused on one home in particular. A big yard for Max and the puppy menagerie they'd acquired. A ready-made pier for the *Now I Sea*. And the Dutch-style home so fun to renovate and restore with her husband.

Amelia rolled her eyes. She'd lost her mind. One moonlight sail and she was ready to renounce her common sense and independence, for what?

For Braeden Scott, of course.

She gulped. Because even a mistaken sighting of said Coastie addled her brain and made her go weak in the knees.

"Amelia!"

She jolted as Victor Kellam, her former high school art teacher and now owner of the exclusive art gallery, touched her arm.

"Mr. Kellam..." Amelia slumped. "You startled me."

The sixtyish retired teacher narrowed his eyes. "You didn't hear me calling your name for the past five minutes?"

She straightened, feeling like the gawky seventeen-year-old she'd been a decade ago. Mr. Kellam had recommended Amelia apply to the Savannah School of Design. He'd supervised Amelia filling out the scholarship application and had taken it hard when she refused the scholarship in order to stay on the Eastern Shore.

"—so pleased with how you've cultivated the natural talent God gave you. I can see the progress you've made since high school. The surety of the line and shadow. I'm thrilled you've finally agreed to show your work."

"What?" Amelia realized Mr. Kellam hadn't stopped talking. "What did you say?"

"Amelia, are you all right? You seem—"

"Line and shadow?"

"The birds are so exquisitely rendered, my dear. As clearly delineated as any photograph. Each feather delicately molded onto the paper. And the ruins of the old lighthouse and village?" His chin quivered. "Haunting. Sublime."

Her mouth fell open. How had Mr. Kellam seen her sketches of the deserted barrier island?

Mr. Kellam continued to wax eloquent. "Friday's local artist gallery stroll is going to be the event of the year with your sketches front and center."

She gasped. "My sketches?"

Mr. Kellam raised his eyebrows. "Amelia, are you listening to anything I've been trying to tell you? After Friday, you're going to be a sensation. The talk of the town."

Her cheeks burned. She'd be the talk of the entire Shore, all right. And none of it good.

Mr. Kellam had always been her biggest fan and supporter in her artistic endeavors. Some endeavors. Now just foolishness with bills to pay and Max to take care of.

The desperateness of their financial situation

yawned once more at the forefront of her mind. A
pit that threatened to swallow her family whole.

She shook her head. "No, Mr. Kellam."

But he ignored her, as he'd ignored her ten years
ago.

"I've sent out mailers. Posted, blogged and
tweeted. Even contacted a friend of mine who's
driving all the way from Baltimore. He's the—"

"You can't do this." Amelia placed her hand
over her heart. Her mouth felt dry as sand. "Those
sketches were never meant for public consumption."

"Your audience is going to eat them up. You'll
have art patrons begging for more. They'll fly off
the—"

"No."

"Amelia, I think your teacher knows best."

Mr. Kellam gave her a look reminiscent of the
one he'd bestowed upon her during her junior year
of high school. He'd overrode her objections and entered one of her pastels into the state fair. At which
she'd won first place and a cash award of fifty dollars.

"It's normal for a person with your artistic tem-
perament to be nervous before a showing. Especially your debut. Totally understandable to want to
hide. But talent like yours must be shared with those
who appreciate your eye for the natural world."

He clicked his tongue against his teeth. "But—
oh, my word, Amelia—the raw emotion, the power
of the seemingly simple—"

"No!"

She staggered. She had to stop this now. Panic lanced her chest until a slow, burning anger took hold.

Who had dared to take her private work—her soul—to Mr. Kellam and induce him to put it on public display? For the entire world to see. To see and laugh. To pity the misguided attempts of the old maid Duer sister to recapture a youthful dream.

"Did Petty Officer Braeden Scott put you up to this, Mr. Kellam?"

Kellam struck a pose. "Petty officer who? It was your father, Amelia. A proud father, I might add, who wants his daughter's talent to get the recognition she deserves."

"My f-father?" She shook her head. "He doesn't know about… I never showed him… It was Mom who encouraged me. He'd be the first to declare my drawings a waste of time."

Victor Kellam stroked his double chin. "I don't know about back then. But as for now, you may not know your father's heart as well as you think you do."

She tightened her lips. "No matter. I won't do it."

"You're going to have to buck up and get over this fit of temper and self-doubt, Amelia." Mr. Kellam folded his arms across his expanded abdomen.

"Excuse me?" She rocked on her heels.

He flung both arms wide. "Are you completely oblivious, or haven't you noticed the full-scale

advertising campaign sponsors have posted on
every telephone pole up and down Highway 13, not
to mention every storefront in a two-county area?"

"I—I…"

She'd noticed nothing. She'd been a gullible, de-
luded ninny preoccupied by moonlit dreams and a
man in a uniform. Busy with salon appointments,
dress fittings, mani-pedis…fishing charters, par-
ent-teacher meetings, not to mention keeping a roof
over everyone's head.

And now to find herself in over her head…up the
inlet in a sailboat without a stroke of wind.

She stamped her foot on the sidewalk.

Mr. Kellam stepped backward. A look of ex-
treme caution—and annoyance—crisscrossed his
florid complexion. "Somebody needs to teach you
to value yourself. To not despise the talent you've
been given. To not waste an opportunity most people—myself included—would die for."

"What're you telling me, Mr. Kellam? There's
no way out of this fine mess Dad's hook, line and
sinkered me into?"

"I'm telling you it's a done deal. No way out now.
Nowhere to hide your talent under a crab pot any
longer. Your secret is out. No recourse but to show
up to the gallery opening Friday night in something a little less—" Kellam gave her a scathing
perusal "—fishing boat. More bohemian. You'll
have to grin and bear the compliments which will

be flooding your way and be prepared to open your bank account for the checks that'll be rolling in."

She choked. "Checks?"

He fluttered a hand. "I take credit cards, too. Deposited into your coffers, after my commission, of course. Which, I'll have you know, is a pittance of what I charge other artists because of our longstanding relationship and because of course I consider you to be my protégée."

Amelia's lips flattened. "Of course."

No worries. No hardworking waterman or -woman would spend real money on such artistic fiddle-faddle. They'd attend as a courtesy to her father. The come-heres, on the other hand? Fair game. And their money, if parted from them, was best left in Eastern Shore hands.

She jutted her chin. "Not even a come-here will waste money on my childish sketches."

"We're going to have to work on that flagging self-confidence of yours." Mr. Kellam threw open the gallery door with a flourish, setting the bells above the entrance a-jingle. "But I'm glad we've got this settled, 'cause like I said, it's a done deal."

She flounced—yeah, a move copied straight out of Honey's playbook—down the sidewalk toward her Jeep.

A done deal with Kellam, perhaps.

But when she got hold of Seth Duer, her father would find out firsthand the true nature of a redhead's temper.

Chapter Nineteen

~❧~

The flyer pinned to the bulletin board at the Four Corners Shopping Center snagged Braeden's attention.

Amelia Duer, Local Artist
Debut Showing
An Eastern Shore Cradle of Life
Friday, Memorial Day Weekend
7:00 p.m.
Tidewater Galleria
Victor Kellam, Proprietor
Onancock, Virginia

What in the world?

Braeden recognized Amelia's masterful touch in the tiny pen-and-ink samples reproduced at the bottom of the flyer. His chest expanded.

He'd make sure the station and the chief knew about the event. The auxiliary volunteers, too.

Between him and her church, she'd have a standing-room-only crowd.

Braeden was a touch surprised she hadn't shared this momentous event with him. The sharing of this most private of things with the outside world. But he felt proud of how far Amelia had traveled from fear to faith.

Faith in God. Faith in herself. And faith in him.

Braeden hoped he'd played a big role in helping Amelia to view herself as he saw her—beautiful, smart, funny and deserving of the best.

This was a big step on Amelia's part. Maybe she'd outgrown the baby steps? Maybe she was ready for the next leg of the voyage. With him.

Still in uniform on a Food Lion run for the guys at the station, Braeden shifted the grocery bags in his arms and headed for his truck. A momentous occasion like this demanded something equally memorable. Amelia could be so touchy, so hardheaded, so...

He sighed. Who was he kidding? He lived to see her smile at him. He never tired of studying every nuance of her features. He wanted a lifetime of laughter with her and Max.

Braeden pointed the nose of his truck south on 13, heading for Kiptohanock.

He'd been waiting for Rawling Miller's check to clear. Pondering how to best approach the situation. The Duers were so independent and proud.

In the meantime, he'd actually taken to studying the real estate listings and the want ads. He'd gone crazy. Certifiable. Nuts. But his heart zinged every time he contemplated a new life with Amelia Duer at the center of his plans.

With the weather warming, it'd soon be time to let Max try his swimming skills off the dock. And there was the much-anticipated Duer family Fourth of July picnic on the island. Honey had told him of the annual Firemen's Carnival, also in July, a Shore tradition in nearby coastal Wachapreague. Seth's mouth watered every time the subject of the carnival's clam burgers came up.

Braeden grinned. He couldn't wait to get a certain Shore girl to the top of the Ferris wheel. He resolved to tell Amelia about selling his boat and—with sharp objects out of reach—share his plan to give Seth time to regain his financial footing. Without giving Amelia any time to bow up, he intended to pledge his undying love and announce his resignation from the Coast Guard.

To be followed, he hoped, by a perfect summer of sand dunes and sea glass with the woman he loved. His heart content for the first time in years, Braeden parked beside the station.

Spotting Seth outside the Sandpiper, Braeden wasted no time in completing his mission. Leaving the groceries for the moment, he hailed the older man, who halted at the sound of Braeden's voice. Catching up to Amelia's father, he drew Seth farther along the wharf for privacy's sake.

But as Braeden opened his mouth, fear slammed

his heart into his breastbone. "Mr. Duer...sir..." Seth Duer leaned against a pier piling and waited. Braeden licked his suddenly dry lips. "I wanted to talk to you about your daughter."

His gaze darted at the cry of a seagull dive-bombing for a fish in the tranquil water off the edge of the dock.

"Which one?" Seth snorted. "Although I could hazard a guess."

"Amelia, sir." Braeden shook his head to clear the cobwebs paralyzing his brain and short-circuiting his tongue. "But first, I wanted to tell you what I've done."

Seth straightened. "This going to require me getting the shotgun out of storage, Scott?"

Braeden's eyes widened. "No." He held up his hand. "Not at all." Though as touchy as the Duers were about handouts... "At least, I hope not."

Seth's eyes narrowed. "You hope? What's this about, son?"

Braeden closed his eyes for a second. He was messing this up royally. "I've sold my boat."

The silence that greeted his announcement dragged Braeden's eyelids open.

Seth knotted his brow. "And...?"

"I have a cashier's check in my pocket for the amount. Which I want to turn over to you to pay off the mortgage on the *Now I Sea*."

Seth crossed his arms. "We don't take charity."

"I—I realize that, sir." Braeden took a deep breath. "But I'm in love with your daughter."

Braeden felt no small measure of relief to finally say the words out loud to Amelia's father.

"And?"

Braeden went into full military stance, feet together, arms clamped to his sides. "I want to marry her, with your blessing. Sir."

"And…?"

Braeden focused his eyes on a pinpoint of marshland across the harbor. "I want to raise Max as my own son, sir."

A chuckle.

His gaze shot to Seth.

"Glad to hear it. But what's this got to do with selling your boat?" Seth uncoiled his arms. "Despite appearances to the contrary, dowries aren't required for our daughters here on the Shore. We're not that old-fashioned. Or is this a bribe?"

"No, sir. Not at all. I—"

Seth's hoarse laugh rang out across the water. "Just joshin' you, boy." He clapped a hand on Braeden's shoulder. "For what it's worth, you have my blessing. You are a fine young man and I'd welcome you into our family."

Braeden fought the sudden tremor in his chin.

Seth threw Braeden a sympathetic look. "But you of all people know that girl of mine's got a mind of her own. Can't rightly answer for her. She's powerfully connected to this place." He sagged. "Though

I've finally done what I should've done a long time ago to push my little shorebird out of the proverbial boat. Sink or swim for it."

Braeden wasn't sure what Seth meant by sink or swim, although that summed up his own philosophy about why he'd chosen this current course of action. "I've also decided not to reenlist."

Seth's eyes enlarged. "What? Braeden, you shouldn't... What about your career, son? You love your job."

Braeden widened his stance into an at-ease position. "Not as much as I love Amelia. She shouldn't have to sacrifice any more of her dreams. Not on my watch, sir. Paying off the mortgage is not a handout but an investment into a new future. I want a life here with her and Max."

Seth's eyes grew misty. "You love her that much?"

Braeden gave a short nod. "I didn't want her to have to make an impossible choice. Not like she did before."

"You know about Jordan?"

Braeden dropped his eyes to the weathered planks of the pier. "Yes, sir. She told me."

"She's not the same insecure girl she was then. And I believe if she'd really loved him, no sacrifice would've been too great to be with him. He was safe. He was comfortable."

"And I'm neither of those." Braeden cut his eyes at the rugged waterman he'd come to admire. "Question is, does she love me?"

"She's like a flower opening to the sun when you walk into a room." Rubbing his sandpaper jawline, Seth smiled, sheepish at his unusually poetic turn of phrase. "She loves you. Real question is whether she'll admit it or allow you to love her back."

"I'm prepared to stick around and show her my sincerity and trustworthiness."

"Always prepared, I'll give you Coasties that. And I've observed you already have a peculiar effect on her independent notions." Seth laughed. "My advice, young man? I'd abandon any plans for a gentle, lapping tide against Amelia's shored-up barriers in favor of a more direct hurricane assault."

"Erode her defenses?"

"Sweep her off her feet like a tsunami. And get ready to employ a boatload of patience. Remember, the best fish are often the hardest to catch. Gotta go deep."

Braeden nodded. "You might be right. You know your daughter best."

Seth grunted. "Have you forgotten practically the first thing I ever said to you, son?"

Braeden cocked his head. "Sir?"

"Don't try to understand women, my boy. All you can do is love 'em. You got that, Coastie?"

A smile teased the corners of Braeden's lips. "Affirmative, sir."

Seth sighed. "Fair winds and following seas, son. You'll need them with Amelia."

* * *

Planting her feet on the planks of the wraparound porch, Amelia set the rocker into furious motion. She watched her dad's truck turn off Seaside Road and into the Duer drive. The tires sprayed a cloud of gravel. Sighting her, her father waved.

A gesture she ignored.

Seth wheeled to his customary spot, rolled the truck to a halt and shifted the gear to Park. He threw open the door and his feet hit the oyster-shell path with a solid *thunk*.

Amelia tightened her mouth.

Seth mounted the porch steps. "Hey, 'Melia. Heard Honey took Max to the video arcade. Thought maybe you and I could grab a coffee in Onancock. Talk some."

Amelia didn't bother to reply. Or to get up.

He gave a nervous chuckle. "Seems a long time since we spent any time together. Had me an idea I wanted to run past you."

She tapped her fingers on the armrest of the rocker.

He blinked. "I remember how you like that French vanilla joe at the Corner Bakery."

She scowled and thrust back the rocker as she rose. "What I don't like is someone going behind my back. You had no right, Dad."

He stepped back. "I—I—"

"I know what you've done, Dad."

Seth backpedaled to a lower step. "How do you—"

"Already been to Onancock today. Begging for another extension from the loan officer. Which the bank refused. Ran into Victor."

Seth rubbed his jaw. "About Victor…"

"Yes, what about Victor Kellam, Dad? The man who's apparently plastered my name and my sketches across every building in two counties." Amelia sank onto the step. "Why, Dad? I don't have time for such foolishness when there's bills to pay. Though after next week—" her head dropped forward "—running the boat won't be an option anymore."

Seth eased down, his joints creaking, beside her. "You deserve more than worrying about mortgages, Max and me." He gulped hard. "I want everyone to see what I already know about my older daughter. What your former art teacher has seen since high school. What I wish I'd taken time to appreciate sooner. To see your talent. See your heart like your mom did before she died. See the hope and promise I believe lies in your future."

Amelia stared at him. "But Dad…you're not well. Max and Honey… The boat? You need—"

"What all of us need is for you to take a good hard look at the wonderful, gifted person God made you to be. You don't have to be the son I never had." Seth sighed. "I should've never made you feel that you did. Instead, you are the best of your mother and me. A beautiful mix of her creativity and my good looks." He grinned to lighten the moment. "'Sides,

I'm not sick. Doc gave me a clean bill of health. I'm ready to go back to fishing full-time."

Amelia leaned against the railing. "That's what I'm trying to tell you, Dad. Next week, there'll be no more boat. No more fishing. No more charters."

Seth patted the pocket of his denim work shirt. "No need for you to fret, Missy. Braeden and I got that covered."

Amelia narrowed her eyes. "What's Braeden got to do with the *Now I Sea*?"

"Braeden gave me the money to pay off the bank loan so we can own the *Now I Sea* free and clear." Seth withdrew an envelope. He handed it to her. "Didn't have time yet to deposit this at the Onancock bank."

Amelia held the envelope between her thumb and forefinger as if the paper might contaminate. "We don't take charity, Dad. Especially not from comeheres and strangers."

"Is Braeden a stranger to us, 'Melia? To you? Is that how you see him?" Amelia flushed and caught her bottom lip between her teeth. "That's what I thought. Anyway, it's not charity. It's an investment. An opportunity he and I have settled between us."

"But how, Dad? Where did a Coastie get that kind of money?"

"He sold his sailboat."

Amelia choked. "He loves that boat. Why would he do that? Why do that for us?"

"Not so much for *us*." Seth smiled. "The why is

his business. Not my story to tell. You want to know why, you better ask him."

"We—I—can't let him do that. He can't sell his boat."

Seth shrugged. "Done deal. Worked out to my satisfaction between us men. What you can do, Amelia, is get off that high horse of yours in thinking can't nobody take care of the Duers but you."

"You've been sick." Amelia bristled. "And I'm not on a—"

"There's no need for you to mollycoddle me, missy. I've recovered from the heart surgery, and I'm anxious to return to the deck of *my* boat. You best be tending to your upcoming art show and the Coastie who—God alone knows why—puts up with your fits of temperamental nonsense."

She swallowed. "About the art show, Dad. I appreciate the thought behind your gesture, but I'm not ready to exhibit my sketches. They aren't good enough."

"Pride or fear, 'Melia. I'm 'twixt and 'tween deciding which of the two will yet be the ruination of you."

Amelia lowered her chin. "And as far as courting a Coastie goes? Probably not a good idea. I lose all common sense when I'm around him."

"Sense isn't as common as you think. And way overrated in my humble opinion." He blew a breath between his lips. "Especially for two people so off the deep end in love."

Amelia flicked a look at her father's weather-beaten countenance. "Love? I never said I—"

"I'm too old for this." Seth heaved to his feet. "Suit yourself, 'Melia, but you may want rethink that by the time Braeden gets off watch tonight."

Chapter Twenty

Amelia waited, perched in the bay window of the front room. She waited long past Max's bedtime for the lights of Braeden's truck to appear.

But to no avail.

Her cheek planted against the fogged-in glass pane, she awoke at midnight to the realization she'd fallen asleep and missed her opportunity.

But there was always tomorrow, to quote another infamous redhead of Broadway fame. She'd waylay Braeden at breakfast and thank him for bailing her family boat out of hock before she lost her nerve.

Unfortunately, Braeden proved a no-show for breakfast, too.

Amelia swallowed her pride. If the ship wouldn't come into port, then the port would go to the ship. But Honey caught Amelia on her way to the cabin.

"I peeked at your schedule. You don't have a charter till this afternoon." Amelia paused in the act of pushing open the screen door. "Dad told me last night about what he's done." Honey blew out an exasperated breath. "How did he think we could get you ready for your debut art show with only a day's notice?"

Amelia grimaced. "I'm not—"

"Don't even start with me, Amelia." Honey held up her hand. "You and I are apparently the last souls on the Shore who didn't know about this shindig. Everybody is coming. You're not getting out of this, not this time. You're going to have to grin and bear the accolades."

Amelia squeezed her eyes tight. "No grinning here. Just bearing it. And I'm not so sure about any accolades."

"I'm sure enough for the both of us. And besides, sister dearest, I got you." Honey nodded. "We're going shopping this morning."

Amelia moaned.

"Yep." Honey smiled. "Something that says artsy, sophisticated and a bit bohemian."

"I've already got a new dress."

Honey arched a look. "That was so last week. It won't kill you to have more than one dress in your vastly neglected wardrobe, Amelia. And a little paint never hurt any ole barn."

Amelia made a face. "You know I don't like—"

"La. La. La. La. La." Honey covered her ears. "I'm going to make a girl out of you, Amelia, if it kills me. And with your attitude, it just might."

Amelia groaned.

Honey wagged her finger. "We're not replaying what you put Debbie, Cindy and the rest of us through with the auxiliary dance. You can either accept my advice gracefully or you can deal with Victor Kellam when you arrive in your cutoffs and Wellingtons. Your choice. Do you want my help or not?"

Amelia made a growling sound in the back of her throat.

Honey squared her shoulders and made an elaborate show of moving toward the stairs.

"Wait…"

Honey ignored her, one hand already grasping the stair railing.

"Please…" Amelia whispered.

Honey clapped her hands together with a delighted laugh. "We're going to have so much fun."

Much to Amelia's surprise, they did.

Honey talked Amelia into purchasing not one but three new dresses. Discounted, but all three Amelia's best colors, or so Honey declared. Perfect for Sunday mornings in church beside Braeden—the part that sold Amelia on Honey's selection.

And those strappy sandals really were as cute as Honey promised. In deference to Amelia's personal taste, Honey managed to find dangly dolphin earrings, too.

"Perfection…" Honey smiled, altogether too pleased with herself. But Amelia had to agree, admiring herself in the mirror at the jewelry counter in Peebles. "Now all you have to do is practice acting artistic and tortured."

Amelia sighed. "The tortured part is going to come easier than you imagine."

Honey sniffed. "This is your night. It's going to be fun, whether you like it or not. So learn to like it."

"I—I—" Amelia studied the overall effect. "I like it."

Honey placed her hand over her chest. "Be still my heart. Have we somehow managed to tap into your inner girlie girl?"

Amelia tossed her head to waggle her new earrings. "I like the jewelry."

Honey laughed. "Who knew all you needed was some bling?"

Amelia fingered the matching filigree bracelet. "It's pretty."

"Like you, sweet sister. Braeden's going to love the new, improved you." She hugged Amelia. "'Cause I happen to know he loves the old tomboy version already."

Amelia raised her eyes. "Do you really think he—he…" Her heart skipped a beat.

Honey embraced Amelia. "What's not to love?"

Braeden gave the sleek hull of *The Trouble with Redheads* one more spit and polish for old times' sake.

"Sure about this, Brae?"

Braeden cut his eyes at the master chief's favorite

niece by marriage, whose husband had just bought the sailboat from him. "I'm sure."

The petite redhead smiled. "This Amelia's a lucky woman to have you in her life."

"Not sure she'll agree with you." He wrinkled his nose. "She's touchy about being beholden."

The master chief folded his arms across his chest. "You've told her about your future career plans?"

"Not yet. But I plan to present my case after the gallery showing tonight. Lay the whole thing out under the glow of moonlight."

Jenn laughed. "Pledging—make that pleading— your troth, huh?"

"Something like that." Braeden grinned. He'd known Jenn and the master chief's entire family for years.

Jenn patted his cheek. "Rawling and I wish you both every happiness in the world."

Braeden glanced around. "Where is your husband and my erstwhile best friend?"

Jenn preened. "My adorable husband insisted on a quick trip to the local grocer to purchase a bon voyage party in a basket as we embark on our maiden sail back to Annapolis."

"Shame my nephew couldn't cut it in the Guard and had to become one of those navy squids."

Jenn poked the master chief with her coral-tipped finger. "You Coastie boys are nothing but a bunch of puddle pirates."

"Hoo-rah!" Braeden and his father's best friend high-fived.

Jenn tossed her hair over her shoulder. "Rawling loves— We both love his teaching assignment at the Naval Academy. Thanks, though, for driving us down so we can cruise back into harbor, Uncle Will."

"My pleasure. Glad it worked out. I needed a word with Braeden anyway. Besides, what else are uncles for?" The master chief flicked a look at his watch. "I've got coffee and a long john with my name on it at the Sandpiper. Senior Chief Thomas awaits to discuss this latest mission directive from District. Soon as I finish, I'll head up 13 toward Maryland."

Braeden wiped a streak of grease off Jenn's cheek. "I assume you and Rawling will rechristen the boat."

She took the cloth out of his hand. "Are you kidding? The name's what sold him on this keelboat of yours. After being married to *moi* for six years—" she squared her shoulders "—he knows firsthand about trouble with redheads. And how ultimately worth it we are."

Braeden made sure he had her attention before he rolled his eyes. He ducked when she threw the cloth at him.

Davis chuckled. "Sorry about the abrupt change of your plans, Braeden. But a temporary emergency change in posting only. Nasty storm headed straight at District Eight, and your senior chief has decided to send any available hands on deck."

Braeden exhaled. "You taught me that from the get-go, Master Chief. The Coast Guard doesn't exist for the Coastie, but the—"

"Coastie for the Guard." Davis's mouth curved.

"Aye, aye. I serve at the Guard's pleasure."

"We need you there, Braeden, ASAP, or Thomas wouldn't be shipping you out tomorrow on such short notice. But with the Category Four hurricane barreling toward the Gulf Coast, stations all along the seaboard are sending any crew and response boats they can spare."

Braeden nodded. "I'll load the boat on the trailer and we'll head out at first light tomorrow."

"I appreciate your flexibility with your enlistment ending so soon. You get this done and I promise not to keep you too long from this lovely place you're determined to call home."

Jenn popped her head out of the galley below-decks. "You'll invite us to the wedding, won't you, Brae?"

Braeden sighed. "If you two would get out of my hair so I can get to a certain gallery showing, perhaps something could be arranged."

Jenn's eyes twinkled.

Davis pursed his lips. "Hate to rush the romance, but—"

Jenn laid her hand upon her brow with a mock groan.

"What?" The master chief's eyebrows arched. "I appreciate heartfelt romance as good as the next man."

Braeden's lips twitched. Shaking her head, Jenn disappeared again below deck.

"Don't be too long about your proposal and good-byes, son." Davis tapped his watch. "You've got places to go. People to rescue. The beginning of the rest of your life to arrange."

Braeden took a deep, cleansing breath.

Starting with one especially stubborn, utterly lovable Shore redhead.

Amelia hunted through her empty portfolio case to assess what her dad—and Kellam—had appropriated for the showing. The bird and wildlife sketches. The barrier island illustrations and—Amelia sucked in a breath at a sudden realization.

She searched the house, but clearly her hiding places weren't such a secret from her father. The pastel of Max at the water's edge with the tiny sailboat—the yet unfulfilled dream of a summer of sea glass, sunshine and sand—was missing.

No matter what Kellam said, that one wasn't for sale. She'd never part with it. She'd sketched the portrait during long hours of chemo infusions. During the wee hours of the morning between holding Max's head over a basin and cleaning up vomit.

The picture symbolized her hope for his future. That drawing was her refuge on the darkest of nights. Faith that summer would come. And with it, new life.

She borrowed a silky mauve blouse from Honey and donned her best pair of jeans. Time to fish or cut bait with Braeden. And—deep breath—ask a certain Coastie to escort her to the gallery showing.

If she could find him.

He'd still not returned to the cabin by lunchtime. Giving herself a few hours before time to pick up Max at school, Amelia stopped by the station.

Behind a monitor, Seaman Apprentice Darden smiled when Amelia strolled inside. "He's not here."

Amelia frowned. Darden laughed. "Am I that obvious?"

"Hard to keep a secret around here. Little-known fact about Coasties? Reason we're so prepared and ready for anything is that we're some of the nosiest folks in the fleet." Darden grinned. "That and it'd be hard to miss the megawattage smile Boats has been sporting since a certain dance." Darden waved her hand. "Yesterday, Boats worked a double shift due to a search and rescue thirty miles off Wacha-preague with a stranded freighter on its way from Cape May to Charleston."

Amelia heaved a sigh. A relief to know he'd not been trying to avoid her.

"He's off duty barring any more emergencies. But I don't know his current location. Sorry." Darden pointed toward the Sandpiper across the square. "Chief Thomas and Master Chief Davis are on a coffee break. If anybody knows where to find Boats, it'd be the master chief."

Amelia's eyebrows rose. "A master chief? Here?"

Darden shrugged. "Old family friend of our executive petty officer. Me? I'm a swamp rat from Louisiana. But with friends in high places like the master chief, Boats is going fast and far."

Thanking her, Amelia made her way into the always-crowded Sandpiper. Amelia nodded to a few watermen who'd returned to harbor with their catch for the day. Honey had asked for the day off in light of the gallery debut.

One of the waitresses put a quarter in the old jukebox. Laughter, conversation and music drifted Amelia's way. Pausing inside the entrance, she scanned the diner. Amelia waved to the pastor's wife and a few other women from church.

She spotted Thomas and—her eyes widened—the silver-haired older gentleman she'd seen Braeden with earlier in the week at Onancock. The men hunched over steaming mugs of coffee in one of the booths overlooking the marina. She moved toward them.

"...with Carly."

Amelia came to an abrupt halt.

"...perfect timing for the XPO..."

Amelia frowned.

"So glad it worked out for him..." Thomas fingered the brim of his cap lying on the table. "But Station Kiptohanock and I will be sorry to lose him."

The master chief nodded. "Like Braeden says, on to bigger and better things."

Chief Thomas took a sip of his coffee. "I can't believe he sold that sailboat of his."

The master chief shook his head. "For the best in the long run. Won't need it where he's headed."

Her heart pounded. Braeden was leaving. Why hadn't he told them? Told her? What was this about Carly? Had Braeden reconciled with his former fiancée?

A sick feeling welled in her gut. She fought a wave of nausea.

"Best thing for everyone. He'll fulfill his obligations." Davis wiped his lips with his napkin. "...strong sense of duty."

Duty? Obligation? Was that Braeden's motivation in offering to pay off the lien on the boat?

Thomas tucked his napkin underneath the saucer. "Quite the catch."

"Last-minute scramble. Change of plans, but—" Davis grinned "—we'll welcome her addition to our family."

Something wasn't right. She didn't understand what she was hearing, but she'd find Braeden. Ask him to explain.

Amelia shifted and the cashier's check crinkled in the pocket of her jeans. And with a sinking feeling, Amelia feared she already did understand. All too well. Guilt money at breaking his promises to the Duers? To Max and her? She shook the flotsam from her brain. He'd made no promises to her. Only silly dreams she'd created in her own mind.

"…he's with her now at the Yacht Club ready to sail away…"

Amelia quivered in shock. Her? Carly? Here?

Was Amelia just another Coastie diversion before he shipped out to bigger and better things? A way to amuse himself for a few months on the Eastern Shore before he returned to Carly?

Her stomach clenched. Maybe the petty officer's pity for the old maid Duer sister no one else wanted? Images raced through her mind.

Ice cream. Church supper. Coffee on the porch.

Shame burned her cheeks. How could she have so misinterpreted his kindness for anything else? Was she so desperate for attention that she'd totally misread his intentions? Her chin dropped to her chest.

Amelia closed her eyes. *Oh, God…*

Her hopes beached on the sandbar of reality. How dare she dream of more? How dare she reach for something beyond her current situation?

What man in his right mind would want to take on her problems, Max and the whole Duer circus? How could she have been so stupid as to trust a Coastie?

Chapter Twenty-One

S wallowing past the bile clogging her throat, Amelia ran toward the door.

"You want something, dearie?" Menu in hand, the waitress approached. Her forehead pinched. "Amelia, you all right, sugar? You look a mite—"

"Amelia?" the master chief angled. "Amelia Duer? Where?"

Panic clutched her heart.

Amelia braced against the door. Shoving it open, she practically fell through it in her haste to escape. Did everyone know about Braeden's plan to leave with Carly?

Scrambling into her car, she wheeled out of the parking lot past a startled Chief Thomas as he and the master chief emerged from the diner.

Thomas raised his hand. "Amelia! I want you to meet—"

Amelia gunned the engine and sped out of town and over the Quinby bridge. As she darted across

Highway 13 bayside, panic gave way to a smoldering anger that he'd so deceived her. Deceived all of them.

Braeden Scott was no better than Max's father. Less honest than Sawyer Kole. He'd toyed with her affections. She might be lonely and pitiable, but she wasn't stupid. She hadn't imagined the moonlight kiss. His flirtations.

Gullible, she'd bought his "rediscovered faith" hook, line and sinker. Good thing he was leaving. Before she'd thrown common sense to the wind and given her heart to the Guardsman with as much foolish consequence as Honey and Lindi.

Amelia rumbled into the parking space at the Yacht Club marina beside Braeden's F-250. Jamming the gear into Park, she hurtled from the car. There at the end of the pier, in the last slip, *The Trouble with Redheads* rode the tide.

Braeden and a woman materialized from below deck. The petite, stylish redhead leaned forward and planted a kiss on Braeden's cheek. Amelia froze.

Carly.

Laughing, he rubbed the spot with his hand. "I'm ready when you are."

She held out her hand. "I've been ready, Braeden, my love."

Braeden rummaged in his uniform pocket and withdrew a set of keys. "Make a trade?"

The woman, on tiptoe, hugged him. "I like how you trade."

"Let the adventure begin." He tossed her the keys, which she caught one-handed. "Here's to the beginning of a brand-new future for the both of us."

She saluted him. "I'll be back. Soon."

Braeden returned her salute. "I'm counting on that. Lots to do before shoving off."

Waggling her fingers, the woman moved away from him and toward Amelia. Jaunty in a wraparound white skirt and navy sailor blouse, the attractive redhead left Amelia feeling overly tall, cloddish and hopelessly outclassed. A wave of expensive perfume preceded the woman, who flicked a languid smile Amelia's way.

Self-conscious of any lingering fish aroma, Amelia shunted aside, giving her a wide berth. The woman's brow puckered, but she crawled into Braeden's truck with an ease that spoke of familiarity and intimacy.

Jealousy slithered across Amelia's raw nerve endings, making it difficult to regain her breath.

Amelia quivered with fury and betrayal. She stalked down the pier to where Braeden busied himself on the deck coiling a rope. At the sound of her footfalls, Braeden pivoted. A smile washed over his face.

Removing the check from her pocket, she flung it at him. Startled, he missed, and the paper fluttered to the edge of the dock to sink beneath the water.

The smile faded from his eyes. "'Melia—"

"I don't want your money."

He straightened. "Look, you need the money. Take it. I explained to Seth—"

"I know about your change of plans."

"Good." He sighed. "Eastern Shore grapevine strikes again. But at least then you know—"

"I know all I ever need to know."

Braeden tilted his head. "It's sudden, I'll grant you. Sprung on me, too. But I planned on coming to the gallery showing tonight to explain."

"Nice of you to tell us goodbye. Better than what Max's father did, taking off without a word."

He blinked. "What're you talking about? Are you comparing me to Max's father?"

"You know exactly what I'm talking about. I overheard the master chief and Chief Thomas talking."

Braeden squinted in the bright midday sun. "You met the master chief, then?"

Her mouth flattened. "What really gets me is how you could lie to a little boy—a little boy who had his hopes disappointed for so long—about being here for him."

Braeden stiffened. "I'd never disappoint Max intentionally, Amelia. This just came up. Maybe by July—"

"I was stupid to let you into Max's life. Into *our* lives."

Grabbing hold of a stanchion, he stepped out of the boat and onto the pier. "Amelia, it's not the end of the world."

Maybe not for him, but for Amelia? The end of

every dawning dream. The end of hope for a life together. She put a hand to her throat. "If you'd only told me you were getting back with Carly, I'd—"

"Carly?" His eyes narrowed. "What exactly do you think you understand about me, Amelia?"

She flung her arm toward the parking lot and his rapidly disappearing Ford. "Here today, gone tomorrow, Coastie. Till you got a better deal. With Carly."

He reared. "That's not who you think it is. Let me—"

"Save it for someone who cares."

His gaze raked her. "After what we've been through together—after all we've meant to each other, or so I thought—I'm stunned by the fact you still have so little faith in me, in us."

Amelia curled her lip. "I'm on to you."

He seized hold of her. "You're really going to walk away? In a fit of temper and pride without letting me explain?"

"Let go of me, Coastie."

Braeden released her arm, one finger at a time. "Have it your way. You always do." He backed away, his hands held in the air. "Shows what fear will do to a person instead of faith." His mouth twisted. "You excel at self-sabotage, Duer. Kind of like what you did with Jordan Crockett, I imagine."

Lunging, she slapped him.

His head snapped, his face etched with confusion and hurt. The sound of her hand against his skin reverberated across the water. He gaped at her. The imprint of her fingers stamped his cheek.

Amelia's palm—and her pride—stung. "Don't you ever compare yourself to him."

"So that's how it is?" Braeden adjusted his jaw with his hand. "Bury your head in the Shore sand, Amelia. My fault for not listening. Two kinds of people here, right? Those like you who stay." A muscle jumped in his cheek, beating a furious tempo. He scowled. "And those like me who can't wait to get away. At least long enough to allow the both of us to cool down from whatever it is you think you believe."

"I believe I hate you, Braeden Scott." She seethed with rage. Ached to smack him again.

His eyes flashed. "You keep telling yourself that, Shore Girl, when you're alone in the moonlight. Maybe a little time stewing in your own juices is best for everyone involved."

He leaped on board *The Trouble with Redheads*. "This has been a whole lot more trouble than I bargained for." She flinched. With a self-deprecating laugh, he stared over the stern toward the open water. "But you're wrong. About me. About everything. Coasties don't quit so easily."

"I've said all I ever intend to say to you, Scott."

Her breath came in short spurts of anger and hurt. She'd never felt like this, even after Jordan died. And if she didn't get away from him this instant, she was going to lose it. She couldn't—wouldn't—allow him to see how deeply he'd wounded her. She refused to let him see her break down.

"Can you not find it in your heart to trust me just a little, Amelia? Please…"

At her noisy silence, the light she'd loved in his chocolate-brown eyes dimmed.

She spun on her heel and raced toward her car.

Braeden didn't call out to her. She didn't expect him to.

Had she not learned at her mother's deathbed the only one you could ultimately depend upon was yourself?

Amelia pointed the Jeep toward home. Trust no one and you'll never be disappointed. That had worked well for her up until the moment she allowed Braeden into her heart. Now she only wanted to crawl into bed and die. Unload her problems onto someone with broader shoulders.

She slammed her palms upon the wheel. She grimaced. Thinking like that had gotten her entangled with Braeden's charms in the first place.

Amelia slackened her death grip. What about her faith? When all else failed, only then did she turn to God? Shame lit on her conscience.

Cast your cares upon Me.

Amelia knew all about casting, except for casting the big stuff. Like Max's illness. Her dad's. Honey's future. Refusing to lessen her grip on her own future, on her own self-directed outcomes.

Suffocating, she cranked down the window. She bypassed the main road and whizzed toward Max's school.

How would she endure the gallery showing? Pretend that all was well when everything most definitely was not well? And never would be again.

Coasting to a stop at the carpool line, Amelia's head fell forward. Pressing her forehead against the steering wheel, she tried to pray, but no words would come.

Life lived in controlling fear was no life at all.

And the overweening anger gave way to a seeping numbness.

Because life without Braeden would be even less of a life than she'd lived before.

Raw pain knifed through Braeden's gut as he watched Amelia reverse the Jeep and drive out of his life forever.

How could he have been so wrong? About her? About a future here?

That Amelia believed he'd choose someone like Carly over her took his breath at how little she trusted him. Trusted in his feelings for her.

Jenn returned with Rawling and found him pacing the length of the dock. She took one look at Braeden, clenching and unclenching his fists, shoulders hunched. "What's that mark on your face?"

Probing his features, she led him away from the water's edge. With Rawling clutching one arm and Jenn the other, they hauled Braeden toward the sailboat.

Braeden gave a hoarse laugh. The sailboat he'd just sold to save Amelia's livelihood. Down payment on a future Amelia didn't want. Not with him anyway. A future he'd so foolishly presumed lay before him.

His mom. His dad. Carly's betrayal.

Why had Braeden dared to dream his future stood a chance of happiness in anything outside the Guard and the sea? Braeden combed his hand over his head.

Rawling tugged him onto the deck of *The Trouble with Redheads*. "You need to take a deep breath and sit down, friend."

"What's happened, Braeden? What's wrong?" Jenn's breath hitched and she cast a look over her shoulder toward the parking lot. "Was that Amelia? Did something—"

"Nothing. That's what happened." Disoriented, Braeden allowed Rawling push him into a seat. "Nothing except my own stupidity. She doesn't... She thinks... I can't believe she—"

His throat constricted. Tears stung his eyes. Braeden gazed across the bay where the water glimmered like diamonds. He squeezed his eyes shut at the reminder of a velvet-lined box stashed in the glove compartment of his truck.

"This woman rejected you after your willingness to give up everything for her? Your boat? Your career?" Jenn's lips bulged. "I'm going to hunt that redheaded Shore woman down and then I'm going to—"

"No." Braeden surged to his feet. "It's over. She made her position clear from the get-go. I hoped..." He gave his friends a bleak expression. "I need to go. Clear my head. Alone."

Rawling touched his shoulder. "Brae, don't. You don't have to go it alone, man. We're here for you. We're always here for you. And when Uncle Will—"

"I'm not going to do anything stupid." Braeden laughed, the sound without mirth. "Nothing any more stupid than I've already done in allowing another redhead to bludgeon my heart—" He darted his eyes at Jenn. "No offense intended."

Jenn hugged him. "No offense taken, Brae." Releasing him, she stepped back. "You go do what you have to do."

Braeden swallowed. "I need to pack my gear at the cabin." His eyes peeled upward at the cawing of one lone seagull that swooped above their heads.

Rawling moved closer. "Go pack, and then bunk with us tonight before you ship out tomorrow."

Braeden shook his head. "No, you guys are sailing with the tide. Maybe Chief Thomas will okay an earlier departure time for me."

He filled his lungs with the briny sea air. And he experienced with a pang of sadness, a measure of young Sawyer Kole's desperation in getting off this strip of land jutting into the Atlantic.

Rawling nodded. "Okay, if that's what you want." His mouth curved downward. "I know you don't believe me now, but this will get better, Brae. With time. Not great, but better once you're out on the open water doing the work for which God has gifted you."

Promising to return as soon as possible, Braeden headed for his truck. Lurching out of the parking lot, he steered toward the highway and crossed over to the ocean side.

Where had God been when Amelia dumped him? Severing his hope and his dream of a new life?

I believed this was the new life You wanted for me, God.

And in the crucible of the moment, Braeden recognized he had a choice—same as Amelia—to trust in God or in himself. To turn away from the God who loved him. Who had always—Braeden saw with the certain clarity of hindsight—been there for him.

With Braeden—whether he'd had the eyes of faith or not to acknowledge His presence. With him when his parents had died, when Carly had betrayed him, when Amelia had transformed his perspective and claimed his heart.

This same God would be there with him during the dark days ahead. While he rescued those in peril from the wind and the waves of the coming storm. While coming to terms with what a life without Amelia and Max meant.

Braeden's mouth trembled at the realization he'd never get to say goodbye to the carrot-topped boy. Or fulfill his promise of a lazy Fourth of July on a deserted barrier island. His chest ached. Perhaps that had been God's intention for Braeden all along in posting him here at Station Kiptohanock? Not a future with Amelia. But to rediscover his faith. To help a brave little boy conquer his fears and overcome a lifetime of pain.

And as for Amelia's fear and pain...

The first rule Braeden had learned in the Guard, which had been reinforced on a nightmarish day in the Florida Keys: save the ones you can. The rest you have to learn to let go.

Braeden traversed the Quinby Bridge and drove a complete three sixty around the Kiptohanock square. He skirted the post office and the Sandpiper. Memories of Amelia and the entire Duer clan assaulted his senses. Driven by a yearning deeper than his unrequited love for Amelia, Braeden pulled into the parking lot of the white-steepled clapboard church.

Kiptohanock...

Faith or fear for the future?

Braeden unfolded from the truck cab. With a desperate longing, he rushed toward the sanctuary. The brass knob moved in his hand, and with a sense of profound relief, he entered the holy place. Found the sanctuary unoccupied and fell to his knees at the front of the altar.

In faith, Braeden chose to believe his time here was more than a matter of killing time before rotating out to a bigger assignment. Here, he'd found the one who loved Braeden most of all. More than any human ever could.

You are the one who loves me forever.

This station was more than just a blip on the trajectory of his career. This fishing hamlet a cornerstone in the evolution of the man God meant for Braeden to be.

Here, with the sunlight dappling the aged wooden floorboards of the century-old church, Braeden chose faith.

Oh, God, faith in whatever You desire for me.

Faith in a future Braeden couldn't envision, but trusted God had in control.

God—not his first love, the sea—remained the only love in his life who hadn't let him down. Would never let him down. And because his God was so good, God had chosen Braeden for a work of great significance. To help others on the sea.

His calling. His purpose. Dust motes danced in the air. Braeden breathed deeply of candle wax and the leather of the big Bible on the altar.

As long as he could hear the crash of the waves, he'd do fine. Better than good now that God reigned in his life. Braeden bowed his head. God…

The only reason a Coastie like him could ever be always prepared and ready. Braeden consoled himself with the thought that women were trouble he didn't need in his Coastie life. But his heart hurt.

And as far as strawberry ice cream, strawberry fields and strawberry blondes?

Head in his hands, Braeden's shoulders shook.

Until a God-planted notion arose. One last act of love he'd not give Amelia the opportunity to reject. Something he prayed God would use in Amelia's heart to work out His purposes, whatever they were for Amelia's life.

Taking a deep breath, Braeden gripped the altar railing and staggered to his feet. One last stop to make in Onancock before he followed his new orders. Leaving his heart behind forever with a Shore girl and a life never meant to be his.

Chapter Twenty-Two

Somehow, Amelia collected Max from school. She'd functioned on automatic pilot since leaving Braeden at the Yacht Club marina.

Scary to realize how little of the drive home she remembered. In the backseat, Max chattered like a squirrel about his and Braeden's big plans for next week when school let out for summer. And he nattered on and on about the much-promised Fourth of July picnic on the barrier island.

Her stomach knotted at having to explain to Max there'd be no picnic. Not for him and Braeden. But she couldn't deal with that now. She'd explain over the weekend. Once this art farce ended.

Somehow she endured the makeup session, surprising Honey with her lack of resistance. She sat still as a statue during Honey's mani-pedi, earning a pleased if confused smile from her.

Honey brandished the hairbrush. "We'll leave it nice and flowing like Braeden—"

"Put it up," Amelia insisted, coming to life for the first time. "In a bun. Tight. Pin and spray it."

And driving toward the gallery as a family, Dad cut his eyes over to Amelia in the front seat.

"Where's Braeden?" Max asked, over and over.

She kept her gaze plastered to the passing highway signs. "I don't know."

Honey caught her dad's eye in the rearview mirror. "I haven't seen Braeden all day."

Seth tightened his hold on the wheel. "I'm sure he'll meet us there. Probably busy with work. But Braeden wouldn't miss Amelia's big night."

Amelia dug her fingernails into her palms.

Reaching over the seat, Honey touched her shoulder. "Are you okay, sis? Nerves are only natural. Don't worry about Braeden. He's never let us—you—down yet. He's probably waiting for us at the gallery."

But he wasn't. As Amelia knew he wouldn't be. Because he'd already let her down in the most fundamental of ways.

The Tidewater Galleria buzzed with snatches of jazz, the clink of glasses and conversation. Victor Kellam had gone all out for his former star pupil. The gallery was filled with friends and quite a few people she'd never met before. Kellam greeted a bearded fiftysomething professor type like long-lost royalty.

Come-heres perused the mounted canvases and

debated the motivation behind Amelia's hitherto secret world. Hors d'oeuvres flew off the trays. Checks were written at a dizzying pace. Victor's assistant affixed sold signs to the dozen or so framed illustrations purchased.

Amelia scanned the two-room gallery for Max's portrait, only to realize Kellam had already sold the pastel.

"Sold," Kellam informed her with an annoyed look in the midst of tallying a receipt for another come-here. "Sold and removed prior to the debut. In this economy, we don't refuse any takers."

Amelia watched the hands of the driftwood clock tick inexorably past eight o'clock. Would this never end? She cast a desperate look around the standing-room-only showing.

With the Memorial Day weekend festival rocking the Onancock marina, the nightlife—and this show—promised to continue until midnight. She calculated her chances of escape. But as the artist in residence, there would be no eleventh-hour reprieve for her from the noisy and intrusive if admiring reviews of her soul on display.

She closed her eyes and longed for the quiet, peaceful barrier island shores. Longed for the lap of the water against the *Now I Sea*. Longed for the summer that would never be.

Amelia swallowed down the yearnings of her heart and once more tried to concentrate on her immediate surroundings. Her reality.

The professor type droned in her ear. Something about birds. "The line and shadowing, remarkable... Have you ever worked in watercolors?"

Perhaps the question was rhetorical, as he rambled on about scope and scale. Amelia's eyes skimmed the crowd, her traitorous heart searching for one face despite her resolutions.

"...glossy readership of over ten thousand. On-line edition more in the range of..."

She spotted her dad talking with a woman from church. One hand clamped on Max's shoulder, Seth anchored the boy in place and out of trouble. She was thankful for small mercies. Max on the loose amid the delicate sea-glass sculptures, paintings and pottery was a nightmare waiting to happen.

"...CEO interested in expanding the line with a print version of the outdated field guide..."

Max chomped on a piece of boiled shrimp. With nothing left but the tail between his teeth, he caught her eye and made an elaborate gesture of puckering his mouth into the shape of a blowfish, as if—

Please don't let him spit the tail onto the floor... not here.

Max grinned at her. And extricated the offending shrimp tail from his mouth with his pinky finger raised—as if sipping from a teacup—he placed it on his glass plate. He winked.

"Just messin' with you, Mimi," he whispered.

She narrowed her eyes at him. Now that he was well—thanks be to God—Amelia had an uncomfortable feeling Max would give her a run for her money. Something she'd have to manage alone.

"When my old buddy Victor called, I never dreamed anyone from this backwater…"

Numb, she rubbed her forehead. Would someone rescue her, please, from this Baltimore art snob?

Honey wove her way through the gathered throng of art lovers. Amelia allowed Honey to pull her into a sheltered corner near the front window. "Headache? Maybe we should loosen the bun, 'Melia."

Amelia shook her head.

Honey waved to the reverend and several waitresses from the diner. "Look—" she pointed out the window "—the Guard contingent has arrived, too."

Amelia tensed as the bell above the entrance jangled.

Like her nerves.

Honey sniffed. "Chief Thomas, I recognize. Darden. Simpson and his wife. But the others…"

Amelia went ramrod stiff as the master chief strolled inside. With Carly. The ultrafeminine redhead poised on the threshold and called to someone on the sidewalk beyond Amelia's line of sight.

Her jaw dropped, and then Amelia closed her mouth with a snap. Braeden Scott had the nerve to come to her gallery showing. And with his fiancée…

Amelia's blood boiled. She clenched her fists.

Honey took hold of her arm. "What's wrong? Talk to me, Amelia."

The redhead pivoted. Arching her brow, the woman slid her hand into the crook of a man's arm. The man she'd apparently been waiting for. The door whooshed shut behind them with another clang of the bell.

But where was Braeden?

Amelia darted her eyes around the gallery. The redhead towed the man toward Amelia, frozen in position beside Honey. "You must be the Amelia Duer I've heard so much about."

Amelia's fingertips sizzled. Braeden had discussed her—them—with Carly?

The redhead extended her hand. "I'm—"

"I know who you are," Amelia rasped, half turning away.

The redhead dropped her hand. "No, I don't think you do. That's why Rawling and I came tonight. I've never seen Braeden so upset."

Amelia flitted a glance at the handsome thirty-something man at the redhead's side. He patted the redhead's hand. "Now, Jenn. Don't go ballistic." He sighed. "Exact reason I'm not renaming the boat."

"Boat?" Amelia took a breath. "Aren't you Carly?"

The redhead sighed. "That's the point. No, I'm not. I'm Jennifer Miller. This is my husband, Rawling Miller, Master Chief Davis's nephew. We've been friends since my husband and Braeden were boys. And today, Rawling bought *The Trouble with Redheads*." Jennifer tapped the lapel of her husband's oxford shirt. "And the boat's name, I promise you, one redhead to another, will be changed one way or the other."

Amelia rocked back. Not Carly. Old friends of Braeden's. Not what she'd thought.

"What's going on here?" Honey grasped Amelia's hand. "Braeden sold his boat? Why? Braeden loves that boat."

Rawling Miller smiled. "'Cause my best friend informs me he loves something—someone—more."

She replayed the conversation she'd overheard between Thomas and the master chief. Could the "her" they'd referred to have been the boat? Not Carly? A sinking feeling threatened to swamp Amelia.

But she'd not misinterpreted his leaving. Amelia stiffened. "I may have got the Carly part wrong. But I wasn't wrong about the here today, gone tomorrow part." She crossed her arms. "Braeden doesn't love me enough to stay."

Jennifer Miller's eyes flashed. "Or you love him enough to go."

"Now, Jenn." Rawling stepped between the women. "It's a temporary emergency reassignment due to the hurricane headed toward the Gulf."

"Haven't you watched the news this week, Amelia?" Jenn maneuvered around him. "Or are you possibly the most self-absorbed human being on the planet? You've broken his heart."

Amelia took a step forward. Honey grabbed her arm.

"Braeden decided not to reenlist." Jenn mirrored Amelia's stance. "He planned to give up his career with the Guard for you." She shouted the last two words.

Heads revolved. An awkward silence followed as conversation ebbed. The master chief broke off from a Coastie grouping and hurried over.

"Clash of the redheads," Rawling murmured at his uncle's raised look. "Amelia's riled Jenn's Irish."

Amelia gaped at Jennifer Miller. "His career? I never asked him—"

Jennifer's lip curled. "You didn't have to ask. That's how much trust he put in your love. His boat. His love. His future."

Seth abandoned the Kiptohanock widow. "What's going on? Amelia?" His gaze ping-ponged. "Honey?"

Honey shook her head. "I'm not sure. Something about Braeden being reassigned. He's leaving. An emergency."

Seth gripped Amelia's arm. "Did you know about this? Is that why you've been so—"

Amelia shook herself free. "I won't let him abandon his career. Not for me. Where—" She whirled, as if expecting Braeden to emerge from the back room.

Davis shook his head. "He planned to ship out at first light, but he asked to head out this evening instead. Said he couldn't wait any longer." Amelia winced. "He was going to pack his things and leave."

Panic slashed her heart.

She'd never told him how she felt. Instead, she'd hurled outrageous accusations at him. He wasn't anything like Max's father. Braeden Scott, willing to sacrifice his boat and his dreams for her, was the finest man she'd ever known.

"I've got to find him." She surged past the master chief and the Millers.

But was there any point in finding him? In stopping him? Telling him— Amelia paused at the door. What would she tell him? That she loved him? Enough to leave her home to go with him?

Hot tears prickled her eyelids.

Someone laid a hand on her shoulder. Amelia turned. Her dad.

"Fight for what you want, 'Melia. If Braeden's what you really want—and I think he is—don't let him go. Don't be afraid." He pressed the car keys into her hand.

Her lips trembled. Fear had always been her problem. She leaned her forehead against the glass door.

She loved Braeden. Loved him enough to go with him?

Oh, God...help me to believe in a future outside these shores. Beyond my fear.

Jennifer Miller touched her hand, locked around the key ring. "Life is always a step of faith, Amelia."

With a quick backward glance over the gathered crowd, Amelia searched the sea of faces. "But Max?"

"Over here, Mimi."

Max perched atop Victor Kellam's immaculate wood-grained eighteenth-century English desk. His Sunday-shoe-clad feet dangled over the side.

Victor grimaced, but made an expansive gesture. "Go. I'm on Max duty till midnight."

Seth wrapped his arm around Honey's waist. "We'll find our own ride home."

Gulping, Amelia pushed open the door and headed for home. Twenty minutes later, she wheeled into the Duer driveway, past the house and toward the wooded cabin.

The cabin lay dark, hunkering in the perimeter of the maritime forest. Amelia flung herself out of the Jeep and hurtled toward the porch. But she knew, even before she yanked open the door, that Braeden was gone.

Already the cabin wore an abandoned, desolate air. Like her heart.

She shook her head and fumbled for the light switch. Not abandoned. She'd driven him away with a lie. The lie that she hated him.

But she didn't hate him. She almost wished she did, because if she truly hated him, her heart wouldn't hurt so bad. A ripping, contorting pain stole her breath.

She stumbled past the small dining table and toward the lone bedroom.

An etched silver picture frame leaned against the doorsill. She sank to her knees with a muffled cry. The portrait of Max at the edge of the tidal creek.

His red head bent over a tiny, furled sailboat. His hand in the act of launching the boat toward a distant shore.

Her hand trembled as her finger traced Max's face and the outline of the barrier island ruins. Amelia plucked the sticky note attached to the side.

"My gift in lieu of summer's promise. Fair winds, Amelia, while I follow the sea."

A sob caught in her throat. Braeden understood how much this painting meant to her. He'd bought the pastel. For her.

Dad had been right—her pride and her fear had been her ruination. She'd lost Braeden's love forever. He was gone.

Chapter Twenty-Three

July 4

The gentle blue-green waters of the tidal creek lapped against the sides of the *Now I Sea* in the soothing cradle of the waves she'd known since birth. A breeze floated past her nose, smelling of sea salt and brine. Her feet rooted to the gritty beach, Amelia tucked a runaway curl into the folds of the flowery purple headband.

Her hair hung long—the way Braeden liked it—and fluttered out behind her like a kite in the wind. Sand crabs skittered in the sand of the deserted barrier island. She tugged at one of the silver hoops gracing her earlobe.

In the month since Braeden had left them—left her—she'd stayed away from this island with its coastal village ruins, only returning today under duress. She no longer craved the isolation of this forgotten shore where she could think her own thoughts. Her thoughts these days were too full of if-onlys and might-have-beens. Nature's beauty failed to soothe the aching restlessness of her heart.

Here she was haunted by everything she'd lost because of her fear and her pride.

Amelia's eyes swept over the rotting stumps of the island dock and the long-abandoned husks of boats moldering at the water's edge. Her paintbrush traced the outline of the remaining stone foundations onto the canvas. Come autumn, in order to fulfill the terms of her illustration contract, she'd have to return and photograph the migratory birds on their stopover to more southern climes.

Beyond the dunes, the ocean waves churned and crashed against the opposite shore. Out of habit, she glanced at the cell phone on her easel before remembering the lack of coverage. But she'd grown accustomed this summer to examining her phone for a text or a missed call.

And every night, she watched the evening news.

The hurricane had decimated the Gulf Coast. Damage was estimated to be in the millions. Coast Guard helos had saved countless lives airlifting victims trapped in flood-ravaged communities. Rapid-response boats performed outright sea rescues from sinking freighters wrecked and grounded by shifting sandbars. She'd monitored the broadcasts, hoping against hope for a glimpse of Braeden using his training and skills to make a difference for those perishing.

She felt as though she was perishing.

And she'd grown accustomed to her dreams being dashed as time passed with no word from Braeden in response to her messages. After a third unanswered message, she'd stopped trying to contact him. Although she couldn't relinquish a stubborn thread of hope that he'd give her—and them—a second chance.

She often thought back to that morning in April—the day Braeden had walked into her life and transformed her world. But after the things she'd said, there was no undoing the damage she'd caused to their relationship. She could only move forward.

The problem was, she'd spent the past few weeks trying to wrap her mind around going forward without Braeden.

She'd promised Max that one fine summer day they would visit the island. They'd have a picnic on the Fourth of July. Hunt for shells. And she'd paint the landscape to her heart's content while Max ran across the dunes. Happy, healthy. Whole.

Not that any of them were happy without Braeden as part of their lives.

Amelia threw the paintbrush onto the tray. She was being paid to do what she loved best. Sketch and paint. But she'd lost the one she loved the most. He'd taken her heart with him when he'd sailed forever out of her life.

Her dad brought Max to the island this summer

when she lacked the heart to do so. Honey hunted for shells with Dad and Max.

On this perfect summer day, the three of them had finally eroded her resolve and brought her here for a family picnic to celebrate the nation's independence.

She'd spent many lonely days and nights grieving Braeden's loss. Falling on her knees and crying out to God in repentance of her pride, her fear, her lack of faith. The weeks provided plenty of time to surrender her illusion of control.

Worse yet? Everywhere on the Shore seemed chock-full of memories, sights and sounds of their time together. She avoided the Coast Guard station like scurvy. She avoided a lot of places in her much-beloved Eastern Shore home. Not so beloved without Braeden in it. Not home—she made the belated discovery—without Braeden to share life with her.

For the thousandth time, she wondered what distant shoreline Braeden currently called home. But wherever Braeden found himself, she prayed for his safety and happiness. Even if that happiness didn't include her. And she prayed with Max, hands folded and knees bent, at bedtime each night.

Because Max insisted Braeden would come back to them. "Braeden promised we'd go sailing to the island, Mimi. We're going to swim. Build sandcastles."

Sunshine. Sea glass. And summer.

From a child's mouth to God's ear. She'd whispered her own silent plea.

Max jutted his jaw in a familiar pose of defiance. "Braeden doesn't break his promises."

Trying to spare his feelings, nonetheless she'd pointed out the unlikelihood of that possibility. Max had told Mimi she needed more faith. But on this holiday of summer, Amelia had yielded her last bit of secret hope and come with them to the island.

A wind-borne shriek drew her attention to where Max chased a sandpiper on the ridge of a dune.

She had Max. Healthy. Swimming off the Duer dock. A regular rescue swimmer in the making, thanks to a certain Coastie.

"Look, Mimi!"

Max waved the large conch shell he'd found. Amelia waved back.

Amelia spotted Honey through the arching fronds of the sea oats as her sister combed for driftwood among the ruins of the lifesaving station. They'd come to a meeting of the minds regarding Honey's future. Honey would take classes at the community college as she wished, save her earnings from the Sandpiper and remain at home to achieve her dream of one day reopening the Duer family lodge as a fisherman's vacation destination. And Charlie Pruitt had come a-courtin', as Seth Duer phrased it.

Yet more than once Amelia had caught Honey gazing off into nothingness, her baby sister's thoughts far away. Because Amelia wasn't the only one nursing wounds and avoiding Station Kiptohanock.

But they had each other and their father.

With fondness, Amelia glanced toward the *Now I Sea* anchored in the crystal cove. Lounging in the captain's chair with the brim of his ball cap pulled over his eyes, Seth propped his feet on the wheel.

Better, stronger, he'd taken back command of the charter business. And begun to spend a great deal of time calling on a certain fellow church member.

A widowed female church member.

"You can't beat 'em, join 'em," Seth muttered when Honey teased him.

The restlessness gripped Amelia once more. Abandoning the canvas, she surged forward. The sand sifted between her toes. The only thing she'd learned that helped was to move and to pray.

Because finally, upon reaching the end of herself and her fears, she had God. Always with her. With Him in her life, she'd never be truly alone.

She'd done a lot of praying for wisdom, for direction—something she should've done much earlier instead of allowing her insecurities, fear and pride to reign over her faith. Time to move forward in faith, to trust God to be enough and to quit wallowing in what wasn't meant to be.

To let go gracefully of what was never meant to be.

Amelia stuffed her feet into her lavender polka-dot flip-flops. Her metamorphosis this summer as she'd embraced her inner girlie girl had been fun, thanks to Honey. And the only bright spot in these weeks of unrequited longing.

She had also begun to draw the attention of former childhood playmates from Little League days. Attention wasted, from Amelia's point of view. Because there was only one man whose attention she yearned for—a Coastie gone from her life as quickly as he'd entered it.

Amelia retrieved the plastic bucket with which Max and Honey had hunted for sea glass earlier. She strolled farther away from the moored *Now I Sea*, pausing now and again to examine a particularly striking shell. Beyond an outcropping of land, blue glass glinted in the sand. She ambled closer.

Bending and then straightening, she held the blue-green glass at eye level and peered through. Her lilac sundress whipped around her legs as a sudden gust of the ever-present wind buffeted a lone white sail rounding the curve of the beach.

Lowering her arm, Amelia blinked, dazzled at the abruptness of the sight. What in the world?

Max shouted from the ridge above. Honey hurried forward and dragged him to the ruined lighthouse and out of Amelia's sight. Amelia swiveled toward the small sailboat. Her eyes widened as the boat drew closer.

Seas the Day, the boat read.

And Braeden Scott, in cargo shorts and a T-shirt, sat at the stern of the boat, his hand on the tiller.

His gaze swept across the beach, zeroed in on Amelia standing stock-still in her tracks and lingered. The tiny sailboat—much, much smaller than *The Trouble with Redheads*—slowed to a standstill as Braeden lowered the mast and dropped anchor.

Amelia's heart pounded at the look in his eyes. Hope, love and faith swelled between them.

Breathing a prayer of thankfulness, she dropped the bucket and started toward the water. She kicked off her flip-flops and plunged into the surf as the current swirled around her ankles. Sliding her feet forward, she went deeper until the water licked at her calves.

"Stop." He held up his hand. "Wait…"

The wind snatched away the rest of his words.

She froze and clenched her fist around the glass fragment clutched in her hand. The glass pierced her skin, but she hardly acknowledged the pain. Amelia's insides twisted.

Had he returned for her? Or only to fulfill his promise to Max?

After dropping anchor, Braeden toed out of his boat shoes. Arching his arms above his head, he dived headfirst off the transom and into the blue-green water.

She held her breath until he emerged from beneath the waves. Turning his face to the side, his long arms ate up the distance between them. He sliced through the water with powerful, steady strokes.

Finding his footing, he rose from the depths of

the inlet. The T-shirt clung to his muscled chest. His dark hair plastered to his head, he swiped his face clear of the rivulets of water streaming down his body. He strode forward, stopping an arm's length away. His gaze never stopped examining her. But his chocolate-brown eyes waited, a trifle wary.

Why didn't he say something? Where had he been these past few weeks? Why hadn't he called?

She dug her toes beneath the warm water to maintain her balance, resisting the pull of the current. But something, long withheld, broke in her heart. Would no longer be denied.

"I love you, Braeden." She gave him a tremulous smile. "I've always loved you. But I've been stupid and cowardly and afraid—"

He made a motion of protest.

"It's true. And I pray you will forgive me for the horrible things I said to you." She swallowed. "As I've prayed to God to give me faith, not fear. For another chance to say to you what's been in my heart." Amelia tightened her hands at her side. "I prayed that you'd return if only so I could tell you—"

"I'm sorry, Amelia."

Her heart plummeted along with her hope. "I—I understand, Braeden." She folded her arms across her chest. "Thank you for not breaking your word to Max about this picnic today. You mean the world to him."

"You misunderstand me, Amelia." His tone bordered on amused. "Seems like we can't stop getting our signals crossed."

Her head snapped up. She flushed, but the expression that flickered across his face reignited her hope.

"I love Max, but I came back because of you. You and me." His voice rasped over his unaccustomed emotion.

"When I didn't hear from you..."

"That's what I'm sorry about. It's been chaotic in the Gulf since the storm. The cell towers were destroyed and communication with the outside world was disrupted."

Her eyes darted toward the *Seas the Day*. "So you went ahead with the sale of *The Trouble with Redheads*?"

Braeden squared his shoulders. "*The Trouble with Redheads* was part of my old life. When you wouldn't accept my gift, I used the money to buy something smaller but still with plenty of room for the three of us." He bit his lip. "Maybe one day, God willing, more than the three of us. Because it was never a question of me loving you. I always intended to return. But it's been a long month of getting my life ready for you and Max. The mission lasted longer than I anticipated."

She rose on her tiptoes in the water. "You love me?"

He sighed. "Shore Girl, how long will it take me to teach you to see yourself as I do?" Tears welled in his eyes. "How long to show you, my darling 'Melia, how much I love you?"

She choked past a half laugh, half sob. "Maybe a lifetime, God willing."

He favored her with a boyish smile. "Didn't I tell you Coasties don't quit?" Then his teeth flashed, buccaneer-style. "We don't give up so easily."

Something broke, the last barrier demolished in her heart.

And suddenly she was done with holding back. Holding back her emotions, her heart, her life.

He'd come back. He loved her. And secure in his love, the barricades of a lifetime washed away.

She opened her palm and allowed the jagged piece of glass to slide out of her hand. The glass dropped with only a small sound into the shimmering blue-green waters she'd loved since birth.

Without a backward glance, Amelia flew across the remaining water dividing them and leaped into his arms. "Miami..." She twined her arms around his neck. "Kodiak..."

He crushed her against him.

Amelia's lips grazed his earlobe. "Wherever the Coast Guard stations you, I want to be there." She brushed her mouth across his jaw. "Because from now on, home for me is where you are. If you'll have me."

The corner of his mouth curved against her cheek.

"Are you proposing to me, Shore Girl? Is this

how you court Coasties? Or is this just how Amelia Duer does things?"

She pulled back to get a better look at his face. He didn't let her drift far, keeping a tight hold on her. She blushed at the teasing look on his face.

Amelia playfully slapped his shoulder. "Don't you dare tell Honey. She'll kill me." She sighed. "I'm afraid this is more how Amelia does things and not so much Eastern Shore."

He laughed. "Well, I happen to love how Amelia Anne Duer does things. Like how she takes care of her family." Braeden leaned in. "Like how she paints and captains a boat. I love how she smells... like key lime pie." He winched a tendril of her hair around his index finger. "I like how her hair feathers in a sea breeze, long and wavy and—"

"And red?" she joked.

His eyes rounded. "I love redheads."

She sniffed. "So you say now."

He unwound her hair from his finger and traced the contours of her cheekbone. "So I'll say forever more." Braeden captured her face in the palm of his hand. "But most of all, my beautiful Shore girl, I'd have to say what I love most about you..."

Amelia's heartbeat accelerated. The eyelet hem of her dress trailed in the tide. "Yes?"

He gave her a smile that made her go weak in the knees. "The thing I love most about you would be your kisses."

She arched her brow. "I don't think you ever

answered my question, Coastie. Answer first. Kisses second."

A muscle in his cheek twitched. He let go of her long enough to rake one hand over his wet Coastie buzz cut. "My answer has always been yes. I have plans to send your family home on the *Now I Sea* this afternoon and ask my own question proper-like under the glow of the moonlight. And I'll have you know I've already spoken with your father."

Now her eyes widened in surprise.

He rolled his eyes. "Yeah. In May."

She cut her eyes to the dunes behind her and across the cove to where the *Now I Sea* anchored. Her father had disappeared discreetly below deck. Honey and Max were nowhere in sight.

Amelia pursed her lips. "And exactly how did you know where to find me today, Braeden Scott?"

He grinned. "I have my sources."

She sputtered. "Do you mean to tell me Beatrice Elizabeth Duer and my father let me moon about—"

"You been mooning over me, Shore Girl?" This time he planted his lips against her cheek. "Good to hear. I've been mooning over you, too." He caressed her cheek with the pad of his thumb. "I came home to you and Max as soon as I could. Took longer than I expected. And I wasn't entirely sure if I'd be welcomed when I set sail today." He took a deep breath. "But I'm not reenlisting, so we can stay here on the Shore with your family. I know how much you love it here."

She shook her head. "No, Braeden. You can't give up your career. Not for me. I won't let you sacrifice yourself."

"It's not a sacrifice to give up something good for something better. My future is with you and Max. To be where you feel happy and safe. I finally found my true home with you and Max in this place." He smiled. "I also heard about your illustration contract. I'm so proud of you letting your talent shine."

"The book contract and the series that follows allowed us to renegotiate the lien on the boat. My art can be done anywhere. And I feel happiest and safest with you."

She attempted to stamp her foot for emphasis, forgetting for a moment the both of them stood knee deep in the water. "You're going to call Master Chief Davis as soon as we get off this island and reup."

"But, Amelia—"

"But nothing."

She placed her hand over his T-shirt, pleased to feel his heartbeat quicken at her touch. "Will you let me do the 'wherever you lead, I'll go' thing or what? It'll be fun."

Braeden cocked his head. "Bossy much, Duer?"

"I'm ready for a new life. With a Coastie. How about you?"

"How many times I have to tell you, Shore Girl, a Coastie's always—"

"Ready," she finished in unison with him.

"You're really going to make this Coastie wait for a kiss in the moonlight?"

"Nah...but you'll make the call later?"

"If that's the price for a kiss, then yes."

She laughed. "How about I show you how much I appreciate your service to your country, Coastie Scott?"

He gave her that lovely, lopsided smile of his. "How about you do that, Shore Girl?"

Amelia's lips parted and his mouth found hers. A sweet fusion of tenderness and joy rocketed into the marrow of Amelia's bones.

"Me-meee!"

Both of them jerked apart. He swung Amelia around to the beach.

Max kicked off his flip-flops. Honey raced after him, yelling her apologies. But as usual, Max was too fast. He beat Honey to the water and splashed his way toward Amelia and Braeden.

"I can hold my breath underwater a long time now, Braeden! I can go deep. Deeper's better."

Amelia planted her hands on her hips. "Max..."

Braeden kept his arms hooked about her waist. "The boy's got the right idea, Mimi. Are you ready to go deep?" His eyes shone upon her with mischief and love.

Amelia nodded. "Like a Coastie, a Coastie's wife is always prepared."

Taking a deep breath, she allowed Braeden to

plunge her into the depths of the blue-green water. Her hair floated like seaweed behind her.

Max dog-paddled to their location and launched himself onto Braeden's back. Braeden tugged Amelia to the surface. He helped her find her footing.

"Do it again." Max wrapped his cornstalk-thin legs around Braeden's torso. "Let's do it again with me." His eyes danced like twin blueberries bobbing on the water.

Braeden rested one hand on Max's kneecap. The other he kept loose around Amelia's shoulder. Braeden's eyebrow rose in a question mark.

"Well?" He grinned at her. "What do you say?"

Amelia snuggled into the two most important men in her world, completing their circle of love.

She smiled at them. "Let's."

* * * * *

Dear Reader,

Thanks for traveling with me to the fictional seaside village of Kiptohanock. The Eastern Shore of Virginia is a real and very dear place to me. I visited the Eastern Shore for the first time at the age of twenty-one. The summer I lived there getting to know the wonderful people and unique culture of the Shore was transformational. And after all these years, I revisit this splendid and unique Tidewater destination as often as I can with my family. Like Amelia, I find peace, tranquility and safe harbor in the Eastern Shore sanctuary of life.

Amelia and Braeden grapple with fears throughout this story. Sometimes things in our past make it difficult to love and trust others. Even God. Especially God. But my prayer for myself and you, dear reader, is that just like Max learning to swim with Braeden, we would be willing to launch out hand in hand with God to the deeper waters where overflowing, abundant blessings await.

I love the Eastern Shore and its people. I hope you have enjoyed taking this journey of faith with me, Amelia, Max and Braeden. I would also love to hear from you. You may email me at lisa@lisacarterauthor.com or visit www.lisacarterauthor.com.

And if you can, hug a Coastie today.

Wishing you all fair winds and following seas,

Lisa Carter

LARGER-PRINT BOOKS!

GET 2 FREE
LARGER-PRINT NOVELS
PLUS 2 FREE
MYSTERY GIFTS

Love Inspired®

SUSPENSE
RIVETING INSPIRATIONAL ROMANCE

Larger-print novels are now available...

REQUEST YOUR FREE BOOKS!
2 FREE WHOLESOME ROMANCE NOVELS
IN LARGER PRINT
PLUS 2
FREE
MYSTERY GIFTS

🌺🌺🌺🌺🌺🌺🌺🌺🌺🌺🌺🌺🌺🌺🌺🌺🌺🌺🌺🌺🌺🌺🌺🌺

HEARTWARMING™

🌾🌾🌾🌾🌾🌾🌾🌾🌾🌾🌾🌾🌾🌾🌾🌾🌾🌾🌾🌾🌾🌾🌾🌾

Wholesome, tender romances

YES! Please send me 2 FREE Harlequin® Heartwarming Larger-Print novels and my 2 FREE mystery gifts (gifts worth about $10). After receiving them, if I don't wish to receive any more books, I can return the shipping statement marked "cancel." If I don't cancel, I will receive 4 brand-new larger-print novels every month and be billed just $4.99 per book in the U.S. or $5.74 per book in Canada. That's a savings of at least 23% off the cover price. It's quite a bargain! Shipping and handling is just 50¢ per book in the U.S. and 75¢ per book in Canada.* I understand that accepting the 2 free books and gifts places me under no obligation to buy anything. I can always return a shipment and cancel at any time. Even if I never buy another book, the two free books and gifts are mine to keep forever.

161/361 IDN F47N

Name _____ (PLEASE PRINT)

Address _____ Apt. #

City _____ State/Prov. _____ Zip/Postal Code

Signature (if under 18, a parent or guardian must sign)

Mail to the **Harlequin® Reader Service:**
IN U.S.A.: P.O. Box 1867, Buffalo, NY 14240-1867
IN CANADA: P.O. Box 609, Fort Erie, Ontario L2A 5X3

* Terms and prices subject to change without notice. Prices do not include applicable taxes. Sales tax applicable in N.Y. Canadian residents will be charged applicable taxes. Offer not valid in Quebec. This offer is limited to one order per household. Not valid for current subscribers to Harlequin Heartwarming larger-print books. All orders subject to credit approval. Credit or debit balances in a customer's account(s) may be offset by any other outstanding balance owed by or to the customer. Please allow 4 to 6 weeks for delivery. Offer available while quantities last.

Your Privacy—The Harlequin® Reader Service is committed to protecting your privacy. Our Privacy Policy is available online at www.ReaderService.com or upon request from the Harlequin Reader Service.

We make a portion of our mailing list available to reputable third parties that offer products we believe may interest you. If you prefer that we not exchange your name with third parties, or if you wish to clarify or modify your communication preferences, please visit us at www.ReaderService.com/consumerschoice or write to us at Harlequin Reader Service Preference Service, P.O. Box 9062, Buffalo, NY 14269. Include your complete name and address.

HWDIR13R

ReaderService.com

Manage your account online!

- Review your order history
- Manage your payments
- Update your address

*We've designed
the Harlequin® Reader Service
website just for you.*

Enjoy all the features!

- Reader excerpts from any series
- Respond to mailings and
  special monthly offers
- Discover new series available to you
- Browse the Bonus Bucks catalog
- Share your feedback

Visit us at:
ReaderService.com